THE HAUNTING

This book is dedicated to my father, Daniel Damon,
who shared my love of scary stories.

The Haunting

The Forest Spirit Series, Book Two

T. Damon

Chapter 1

The Nymph Palace stood triumphantly within the cliffside, the formidable roots of the centuries-old oak tree drooping down to gently tickle the earth with its own version of fingertips. Within the palace, only slight reflections of sparkle shimmered from the limestone and quartz forged into the walls. Good energy once radiated here not long ago, but now the feeling of impending tragedy was impossible to ignore.

King Alston, ruler of Nymph Kingdom, had been targeted foremost by a force backed in an unyielding strength of will. His only son, Rowan, led the crusade of darkness against his own father, mother, and his very kind, just a mere generation after Alston considered himself rid of the nuisance of a potentially negative threat.

Rowan stripped Alston of his throne, and enslaved the king and queen to his accord. No longer would Rowan call Alston his father, but then, no longer was Rowan a being of light. He was infinitely transformed by the falling, and submitted so deeply to the hatred that boiled within his soul that he could no longer be saved. Not by the Higher Spirits, not by his loved ones, and certainly not by himself.

"Do you know how long I have waited for this moment, Alston?" Rowan sneered as he sat upon his father's throne, looking down at his creator who was kneeling on the ground with his eyes lowered. His wife, Queen Tiatana, knelt solemnly beside him.

Alston peered up at his son. "No, my son," he nearly whispered. "Twenty years?"

"There is no sense of time or space where I came from. I assume it's been about a generation or so. But how am I to know?" Rowan griped. "I've been rotting in the underworld while you gallivant about, pretending to live a harmonious life, pretending you actually cared enough to try to save your son's soul."

Indeed, Rowan did appear to be rotting. His eyes were sunk deep into his skull, and his flesh was torn down his cheeks as if he had clawed his pointed fingernails from temple to chin. His complexion was dull, lackluster, and muddy, and his hair was matted and spiked across his head, soaked in dirt and moisturized in blood.

"But the time has actually been good to me, as it allowed me to build up enough energy to become more powerful." Rowan got up from the throne and began to encircle his father. "My entire existence I spent living in your shadow. But just look at me now. I've become the shadow!" He laughed maniacally for a moment, then suddenly snapped back to a stoic glare. "I spent all these years held captive by the entities of the underworld, waiting to enact my revenge upon the beings of light. Revenge, upon the very nymph that gave me life. A life I now wish I never had. You, Alston."

"I never meant for it to be like this, Rowan. For that I am eternally sorry to you," Alston said, sadness heavy in his voice.

"It's too late for that," Rowan replied angrily. "Now you will feel what it is like to be enslaved by the darkness, just as I was. But this time, I am the darkness!"

Rowan seemed far away for a moment, then suddenly snapped back to reality. He walked back to the throne and sat down upon it, glaring at his parents. He instantly became so overwhelmed with anger and hatred towards them that he pulled his own dagger out of his pocket, and rose up from his seat once again to wave the blade in his father's face.

"What are you going to do, Rowan?" Alston asked, his voice forceful but with a softened undertone. "Are you going to kill me?"

Rowan laughed. "Why wouldn't I? After all you've done for me," he said sarcastically, walking behind Alston and pressing the tip of the blade into his back. "Just one powerful thrust, and this dagger will pierce straight through your heart."

"Please, Rowan!" Tiatana called out in desperation. "We love you!"

"I know you may have at some time, Mother," Rowan replied calmly. "But Alston is another story." He looked at his father. "Well? Do you love me?"

Alston seemed taken aback. "Of course," he whispered.

Rowan's face hardened. "I don't believe you," he said, and clapped his hands twice. "Caul! Caul, get in here."

A monstrous, writhing, ashy-colored creature slid, hunched over, into the room. Though slightly larger than Rowan, the creature's posture made it appear as though he were in submission to the rotting nymph. His eyes, sullen and gray, did not yield from his master, his soul controlled by a desire to obey a being more powerful than himself. The creature was a goblin, a member of a former kingdom that lost its standing in the Forest by submitting fully to the negativity of Gorgon, and pushed out by the armies of light many generations ago. If the Higher Spirits no longer looked upon the goblins with enough favor to preserve their existences within a kingdom, then surely no good could ever come of them joining an entity whose intentions were so backed in apathy and hatred for love.

"Yes, my liege?" the goblin hissed, bowing to Rowan.

"Remove this mess from my sight," Rowan sighed.

"Mess?" the goblin questioned, seeming confused.

"These two, Caul. The king and queen. Dispose of the king, and lock the queen in the back quarters."

"How would you like me to dispose of him?" Caul replied.

Rowan tossed the goblin his dagger. "Bring this back to me when you're done. With his blood still fresh upon it."

Tiatana gasped, but Caul giggled. "Very well, my liege." He screeched an ear-piercing scream, and two more goblins rushed into the room, grabbing the queen and dragging her away.

"No!" Tiatana yelled. "Rowan, please!"

"Goodbye, Mother," Rowan said, sounding bored. "If she resists, kill her."

Caul snatched up Alston with the help of the other goblin, and the two pulled him out of the room as he struggled for his life. A few moments later, Caul returned, and handed Rowan his bloodied dagger.

"The deed is done, my liege," the goblin said.

Rowan studied the dagger for a moment, and slid his finger over the deep, crimson red that stained the blade. He placed it by his side and looked up at Caul, smiling. He picked up Alston's crown that had been sitting beside the throne since Rowan overthrew him and delicately dropped it down upon his head.

"Now, bow to your new king."

The Haunting

True harmony can only exist when all in question are willing to accept the light of love in their lives. Thus, a Forest, once so ripe with living beings breathing the rich, clean air, once again becomes engulfed by the thick, eerie fog that suffocates those who gasp for righteous breath. Blackened is the dirt, and twisted are the trees, and yet one would not even ascertain that anything was awry without the deep-seated intuition that comes along with existing as a being of light within this realm.

A Forest, which just a generation ago was beaming in harmony, now has turned to a more sinister feeling, seething with negativity that lay dormant for enough time for the beings of the Forest to nearly forget their harrowing history.

The time of the haunting did not begin at Nymph Palace; but rather, it started a generation ago around the very time that Rowan, son of King Alston, perished at the hands of Labete's possessed insects. Coincidence? Not likely. This Forest is one of serendipitous synchronicity, not a place where any strange occurrence can simply be explained away by coincidence. The Forest's spiritual bindings had been weakened, and opportunists of this sort tend to be attracted to such suffering. And yet, fate is a determined fury, and whatever is meant to be will come to fruition one way or another.

No longer will Rowan call Alston his father; but then, no longer is Rowan a being of light. He was infinitely transformed by the falling, and submitted so deeply to the hatred that boiled within his soul that he can no longer be saved. Not by the Higher Spirits, not by his loved ones, and certainly not by himself.

CHAPTER 2

"Come on, Eleonora! We're almost there!" Felix Hawthorne, an orange-eyed warrior nymph motioned for his good friend, faery warrior Eleonora, to follow him into a thick patch of trees on the northernmost end of the Forest.

"Hold on a second, would you?" Eleonora's bright, teal eyes met with her friend's. She paused for a moment, smoothed her soft hands over her iridescent wings, and fluttered briskly to catch up with Felix. Her chestnut brown hair fell gently over her left eye, and swooped across her beautiful glowing face, curling upwards in a dangling bob. Faeries have a way of sparkling as they move about, and Eleonora fit the profile very well.

"Wait for me!" Eleonora soared quickly over to Felix, catching a slight wind to move her along faster.

"If we arrive late, we'll miss the good part!" Felix held his hand in the air, silently requesting that his faery friend descend to the ground to walk beside him. Eleonora drifted down slowly and grabbed Felix's hand.

The two cleared their way under a berry bush and approached a bright clearing filled with flowers of varying colors and heights, amidst the thick growth of trees and bushes. They entered the clearing, and Felix led the faery to a young oak tree that had sprouted in the very center of the clearing, growing freely out of a scorched, humanoid shape that was burned into the soil.

Felix and Eleonora reached the sprouted oak, studied it for a brief moment, then gazed at the clear blue sky above, unable to hide their excitement at some alone time with each other, and both praising their fates that they were able to connect on such a lovely day.

"What a beautiful morning!" Eleonora commented, rightfully so, as the day had emerged from the darkness of night gracefully, and the trees surrounding the clearing seemed to sing the praises of such a gorgeous day. It was early morning, and Felix had woken his friend and guided her out of their station in Troll Kingdom to witness something that only happened once a year.

Felix and Eleonora were no strangers to the darkness that dwelt in the undertones of the Forest. As warriors, protectors of the land, they had learned of the many forms of darkness in their time, though had scarcely experienced it themselves. They were stationed together in Troll Kingdom, Felix by order of King Alston himself, and both took their positions very seriously. This morning, however, their venture into the clearing was one of pleasure, not assignment. Felix knew of a breathtaking occurrence that was to take place in just a moment, and wanted nothing more than to share the experience with his closest friend.

"The morning is indeed beautiful, and all the more lovely when I get to share it with such an amazing being!" Felix beamed at the faery.

Felix was small in stature, like his mother Narena, and inherited not only her eye color, but her thirst for adventure and knowledge. Though much like his father, Kellen, he gained a practical mind and the true heart of a warrior—not to mention striking good looks, dark brown hair and chiseled musculature. As per his own request, he was stationed in Troll Kingdom by his king to keep order in that section of the Forest, but had always secretly hoped to experience the same kind of adventure that his parents had not long before his mother gave birth to him. That is, of course, until he met Eleonora, when nearly all of his aspirations for his own excitement went out the window, and his goals and dreams began to include the exquisite female faery as well.

Felix had always made a point to treat every being in the Forest with the utmost respect, as the tales of his parents' adventures bore deep into his mind from a very young age. Eleonora respected this immensely, and took as a personal example for herself on how to act. Felix and Eleonora, though aware of their feelings toward one another, had decided aside from the other that they would not act on their feelings, as the Forest was still not currently in a state where a nymph and faery warrior could outwardly express their emotions for one another unless under a special circumstance, like the one surrounding Felix's uncle, Nyxen, and his faery wife, Sebillon.

But Felix's intuition was nearly spot-on, much like his sage mother, and he couldn't help feeling that despite the beautiful day, something was seething beneath the Forest floor. In addition, he was starting to notice a slight headache that pierced into the frontal lobe of his brain, and was now slowly beginning to span across the width of his entire head. Now was not the time for a headache, however, so he tried his best to to ignore it.

"So what are we here for, anyway?" Eleonora said, squinting her eyes to peer at Felix.

"Just wait another moment, you'll see," Felix replied. He beamed at his friend, slightly blushing as he gazed at her face, her eyes wide in excitement and anticipation.

The clearing grew brighter as the sun positioned itself to perfectly shine down upon the young oak tree, and as they looked closer, they began to notice small, light green seed pods begin to vibrate slightly. As they moved even closer to the tree, they saw that they weren't in fact seed pods, but tiny cocoons that shook around until they split open. Little black heads burst forth, attached to long, thin antennas that curled around in circles, feeling the fresh morning air for the first time in new bodies.

Stunningly bright orange and yellow wings pulled their way out of the cocoons, whirling around to quickly dry off in the sunshine. After their wings had dried, the butterflies took off into flight, testing out their new fluttering skills in the clearing, stopping every once in awhile on a brightly colored flower to imbibe nutrients before their next journey.

Felix and Eleonora watched in amazement as the clearing, which had been so silent and dormant upon arrival, became a whirling, bustling butterfly garden. The insects fluttered about, so closely to the nymph and faery that the two could feel light wisps of air graze their cheeks as the butterflies swooped by them.

"This is amazing!" Eleonora shrieked in delight.

"Isn't it?" Felix beamed, and clutched onto Eleonora's hand, unknowing of the bright red hue his face had involuntarily flushed, but not seeming to care about it in the slightest. "I knew you'd enjoy it!"

"Know what I read about butterflies? Some of the native humans believe that they carry souls of the dead, and seeing them like this is surely a good omen!" Eleonora grinned at Felix, and he back at her, proud that he knew such a bright and vivacious individual.

Eleonora closed her eyes and whirled around in circles, laughing and swinging Felix around with her, so fast that the colors of the butterflies and flowers to them became a blur. Finally, the butterflies took off, heading south, out of the clearing and into the Forest. Eleonora and Felix stopped twirling and watched as the fluttering wings flew further and further away from them, becoming tiny specks of orange and yellow, before disappearing completely from view.

The two walked back to Troll Kingdom, excitedly skipping their way through the Forest until they reached their station within a large stretch of rock quarry, and checked in for the day with a very annoyed looking male faery.

"You're late to report, you know," he scowled at them, furrowing his thick eyebrows and squinting his eyes at his returning comrades.

"Sorry, Garmon," Felix replied. Eleonora nodded. Garmon was not one to tolerate any form of nonsense, as his status as the leader of this particular sector of the Troll Kingdom station didn't provide any room for shenanigans.

"Do you know how hard I've worked to gain the status I currently hold?" Garmon asked, annoyed. His gaze softened a bit when it fell on Eleonora. "You were due to report ten minutes ago. Everyone is waiting for you."

"I said we were sorry," Felix grumbled. He was after all, his father's son.

"Yes, we do apologize, Garmon. We didn't mean to be late," Eleonora chimed in.

"Fine, fine," Garmon replied. "Just get to your morning exercises."

Garmon was tall for a faery, and had wide hazel eyes which spanned across his long face around a sharply angled nose. He had dirty blond hair which barely hung over his pointed ears, wide shoulders and chest, and thick, muscular arms. He was skilled in the art of spear throwing, and considered among the best throughout the entire Forest, something he was known for sharing in great detail with anyone and everyone who was willing to listen. But Garmon was indeed a great spear thrower, and continually had proved himself time and time again, so despite his pompous nature and propensity for bragging, there was still no arguing that fact.

Felix and Eleonora headed to their training exercises, as Garmon carefully folded his wings behind his back and slowly followed behind. When they arrived at their training area, they joined a group of individuals from various species, all sent to Troll Kingdom for the same purpose: protect and keep guard over the northernmost end of the Forest, and report any signs of another impeding situation like the falling.

Felix and Eleonora tried their hardest to avoid eye contact with each other as they stretched and practiced some spear-throwing and archery, as they knew if they so much as glanced at one another that it was possible they might burst out into uncontrollable laughter at Garmon's never-ceasing grumpy demeanor. Felix's accuracy was near perfect on this particular day, and he thought to himself that Garmon's ornery behavior just might be the kick that he needed to really impress Eleonora with his skills. Felix could only assume that having the female faery around him as he practiced, constantly on the verge of giggling to each other about an inside joke, only made him a better warrior.

When morning exercises had ended and all the warriors had quenched their thirsts, Garmon called the army to gather around him for a meeting.

"All right, everyone, let's gather round so we can discuss our most recent events," Garmon called his multi-species army to his side, making a point to stare just a bit longer at Felix and Eleonora.

A dozen or so individuals, mostly faeries, trolls, and a few Forest animals, like birds, toads, foxes, and a skunk, encircled Garmon and anxiously awaited his morning announcements. Felix was the only nymph stationed in Troll Kingdom, something he prided himself on, as Troll Kingdom was quite a ways away from his kingdom of birth, and—given the location of Troll Kingdom—was a station that included some of the best warriors in all of the Forest.

"Just this morning I received some harrowing news. Alston, king of Nymph Kingdom, apparently perished in his palace just last night. I received word by way of a messenger crow who flew the information to us. Felix, you will need to return to your kingdom immediately. I would like a few volunteers to accompany him, and ensure that everything is all right in Nymph Kingdom before returning here. Who would like to volunteer?" Garmon's eyes scanned across his army.

"I will, Garmon," Eleonora instantly replied, much to Garmon's dismay. He rolled his eyes in disgust.

"Of course you will, Eleonora," he replied with a groan. "Anyone else?"

"I would also like to accompany them. I've always wanted to see Nymph Kingdom, I've heard many tales of the land," replied a male troll with jet black hair and lavender eyes.

The troll was large, much larger than a nymph, about the size of a deer's head. If provoked, he had the ability to puff up his body to appear much larger in order to intimidate his foes. But trolls were generally thoughtful beings, and would prefer the practicality of conflict resolution to that of challenging physically, despite their inherent tempers. This particular troll had made a name for himself in his kingdom with his outspokenness and overall intelligence. Though extremely strong-willed, he was, in his heart, a very kind individual.

"As you wish, Myso. I will also come along, as you will no doubt need some extra guidance and protection that can only be provided by someone with much experience," Garmon said, looking quite proud of himself. "Gorgon might see us as weak and send more tribulations our way if you are not led by a formidable being."

"I'm sure the Yew looks favorably upon Felix," Eleonora said quietly, though not loud enough to pique Garmon's interest. If he had heard her comment, he chose to ignore it.

Felix turned his head away from the group to make a face at Eleonora, who noticed it and tried to hide her laughter.

"Something funny, Eleonora?" Garmon shot his eyes over to the faery, but his glance was not harsh.

"No, sir, all is well," she replied, but couldn't hide the residual smirk that stretched across her face. Felix covered his mouth to conceal his smile.

"Very good, then. Basil, if you wouldn't mind, I'd like you to come as well. Just in case our little nymph warrior's feet get tired," Garmon said, cocking his head in Felix's direction.

The skunk poked his furry face above the crowd and nodded at the faery, then exchanged an excited, goofy smirk with his best friend, Myso the troll, who beamed at him in return.

"With all due respect to Basil, I must say that my feet will do just as well as wings," Felix snapped, irritated at Garmon for calling out what he felt was his only weakness as a warrior—and something that he, as a nymph, did not have any control over.

"It's quite all right, Felix, I really don't mind coming along," Basil replied hurriedly, trying to put an end to the escalating confrontation between the nymph and faery. Upon hearing Basil's words, Felix immediately calmed down, and did so further when Eleonora rubbed her hand across his back comfortingly.

Basil was quite normal as far as skunks were concerned. He was typical size and coloring, and from an outward perspective there was nothing terribly exciting about the animal, except for the fact that he was the sole mustelid in the Troll Kingdom army. Basil had worked hard for his status, amid discrimination from other species' kingdoms that were keen on questioning his abilities as a warrior due to his penchant for using the stench of his musk as his go-to defense mechanism.

"All right then, prepare yourselves to leave at once. Meet back here in an hour," Garmon said, and the gathering dissipated.

Felix stormed away with Eleonora close behind. "Can you believe him?" he hissed to the faery as they walked. "I don't think that miserable being could be more wretched if he tried."

"Oh, don't say that," Eleonora replied with a wink. "I'm sure he could be."

"You're probably right," Felix mumbled. "He would probably do everything in his power to stop me from achieving any kind of accomplishment like my parents."

"Well, don't you want to make a name for yourself?" Eleonora asked. "You have your own life to live. You can't just string along behind your parents. You're destined for great things by your own accord, Felix, I'm sure of it."

Felix beamed at Eleonora. "You always know how to make me feel better," he said softly as he brushed his hand against hers, wishing to grab tightly upon it but not confident enough to fully commit to the hold. Eleonora seemed not to notice, and kept her pace shoulder to shoulder with Felix.

Nymph and faery unions were not something that was typically smiled upon within this particular Forest. Though it was encouraged for all species to live harmoniously, there were a few unspoken taboos within these trees, one of which was that nymphs and faeries were forbidden to marry. Prior to the recent falling, practically no one broke the taboo, and if anyone did it certainly was not spoken about or well known in any given community. But Felix's uncle, Nyxen, and aunt, Sebillon, were pioneers at the forefront of breaking this rule, something Felix reminded himself of any time he felt patronized by Garmon.

Nyxen and Sebillon's union was acknowledged only after they risked their lives for the good of the Forest, and returned victorious and subsequently, in love. They chose to live in Faery Kingdom to appease Sebillon's family, as faeries were much more opposed to nymph-faery unions than the nymphs were. Their union was only accepted by the faeries after describing their harrowing journey, as well as their gradual fall to love, to the Faery King, Laurel. And after Sebillon gave birth to a daughter bearing faery wings, the kingdom had officially declared that they approved of the marriage.

When nymphs and faeries reproduce, the possibility is left open of whether the child will be a little more nymph-like, or a bit more faery-like; but it varies depending on the couple, and by social standards. Nyxen and Sebillon's child was extremely gifted to be born with wings—by Faery Kingdom standards, that is. If the child had been born more nymph-like, it's very possible that the couple would have been excommunicated back to Nymph Kingdom.

King Alston, though riddled with faults, did have one very progressive view about the Forest. Though he never spoke much of it, he turned a blind eye as he did with most matters of the Forest. He allowed nymphs and faeries to intermarry—though *allow* is a generous term, as it was unknown as to whether he actually did in fact allow it, or he simply did not care enough to take a stance on the matter.

Either way, Nymph Kingdom became known in the Forest as an area to which acceptance, or obliviousness, was more apparent than the others. Felix knew, one day, that he would once again reside in the kingdom he grew up in. But for now, he could only hope for adventure, and trust in his love for Eleonora, for someday they would possibly live in Nymph Kingdom together. That is, if Felix succeeded in impressing her enough to marry him.

Felix went to his quarters and prepared his satchel to leave, packing what few items he had. A blade, a spear, a bow and arrows, a candle, an extra tunic, some food, and water droplets rolled into leaves.

Eleonora also packed her things at her bunk, and when she was done the two reconvened and walked back to the meeting spot together. Garmon, Myso, and Basil were already there, waiting for them to arrive.

"Are we all ready, then?" Garmon asked curtly.

"I believe so," Felix replied, and tried to smile at the male faery, who looked very quickly at him then dashed his eyes away and stuck his nose in the air.

"Then we are off!" Garmon declared, and marched ahead of the group, head held high, out of Troll Kingdom and into the Forest, unknowing of what was to come, yet seemingly not caring of his fate in the slightest.

CHAPTER 3

Back in Nymph Kingdom, goblins were slowly trickling into the palace, called by Rowan and his goblin henchman, Caul, to overrun the kingdom and overtake any authority who stood in their way. Rowan allowed the goblins free run of the palace, and they took quickly to their inherent destructive nature.

"I will be in Alston's quarters if anybody needs me," Rowan snapped at Caul. "Or should I say, *my* quarters now."

"Very well, sire," Caul hissed in reply.

Rowan made his way to his father's quarters and quickly began tearing apart the room, searching for any book he could find on magic. His mother, Tiatana, sat tied to her late husband's favorite chair, her long blonde locks cascading down her face as she hung her once-sparkling eyes to the ground, unable to see what Rowan was doing though hearing noises behind her.

"What are you searching for, my son?" she asked nervously.

"That, Mother, is none of your business," Rowan said. "And you would be wise to hold your tongue in the presence of the king, lest you be willing to face the fate of your husband."

"My husband was your father, Rowan," Tiatana replied softly. "What happened to my sweet boy? You are no longer the child I carried in my womb."

Indeed, Rowan had changed quite a bit in the last twenty years. A long time had passed since Rowan was a nymph, though he was once a very handsome one at that. Son of royalty, a competent warrior, and with striking good looks genetically inherited from both parents, Rowan seemed destined for greatness from a very young age.

His eyes, which were once a sparkling blue to rival the ocean waves, were now glazed over, a dreary shade of bluish gray. His golden hair, now matted, did not resemble the style of its once-living counterpart. Rowan was a shell of his former self, and though his former existence had harbored a similarly bad attitude, there had still been a hint of good that dwelt within him. That bit of good was now gone, drowned by the darkness and swallowed into the nether-regions of all that is long forgotten.

All of Nymph Kingdom was aware that Rowan was fated to one day wear the crown and bear the burden of the kingdom as leader, but nobody assumed it would be under such circumstances. The nymphs hoped, in all their blind faith and possible obliviousness, that Rowan could perhaps be a different king than Alston was. They also wished fervently to the Higher Spirits, on many a clear, starry, summer night, after a fine evening of socializing at the Holly Bush Pub, that Rowan could lead the nymphs to become a more caring and involved society of the Forest. But that hope, that last clinging bit of faith, was now gone, destroyed by Rowan's death and fall to the darkness. The falling had long ended, and yet the suffering of the Forest was still imminent.

"What happened to me? *What happened to me?!*"

Rowan violently threw a pile of books onto the ground, and stormed over to the chair, standing directly in front of his mother, his putrid breath hot on her flawless face. It smelled as though a dead, rotting rodent had crawled into his mouth and proceeded to live under his decaying tongue for several years, sustaining itself on a diet of pure excrement.

Tiatana couldn't help but cringe, which caused her son to cackle and mock her, so the queen continued to avert her eyes, knowing that if she were to fully face the creature that was once her son, her ability to withhold her tears would fail. She knew what Rowan had become, so to the former nymph, mercy and sympathy were no longer comprehensible.

Tiatana was a strong female nymph, and willful in her own right, as being married to a being as stubborn as Alston would surely require such a personality. She did not always necessarily agree with her husband's methods of rule; yet she'd learned early on in their marriage to hold her tongue in the presence of a male superior, especially her husband, who did not always look with favor upon an outspoken female. And since she had wanted nothing else in her existence but to marry well in terms of wealth and status, she was willing to do everything in her power to maintain her position as queen. Over time she had learned, in her own way, to manipulate Alston to some degree, using her gorgeous looks and feminine wiles to sway him in her direction, even if only slightly. But this situation was one far beyond her control.

"You want to know what happened to me? I experienced no love from you, not a pinch of such to save my soul. I gave up any remaining hope I had for the goodness of my own kind, and fully submitted to the darkness. For years I clutched onto my last vestiges of consciousness in that torturous underworld, and I came through. I tore my way up, back to your realm, and swore I'd seek revenge on those who had forgotten me. You, Mother, are merely a casualty in my quest for destruction. And if you get in my way, I swear to you I cannot prevent the gruesome outcome that the goblins will bestow upon you. Trust in me that you will beg for your death." Rowan glared daggers into his mother's eyes, the eyes that so resembled his own.

"Rowan, I do not know why you say you experienced no love from me, for I loved you with every inch of my being. You're my son, my child, my baby. I loved you from the moment I was aware of my pregnancy, and I still love you to this very moment," Tiatana said, choking back tears.

Rowan laughed. "Well, you have a funny way of showing you love, don't you, Mother?"

"Rowan, please. Don't do this. I beg of you."

"Begging is a good place to start."

Tiatana stared at her son for a moment, not in the slightest recognizing him as the child she carried and raised to one day be king. True, Rowan had always been difficult—the son of a king was almost surely to be spoiled in some way which could taint his outlook on life in general—but as Tiatana recalled the time of her son's childhood, she realized that his rage and anger had seemed be a deep-seated ruler of his soul.

Rowan had been prone to throw a tantrum at the slightest mishap, quickly become angry at helpers in the palace whom he felt were below him, and even talk back to his own parents, who had always been apt to ignore their son's behaviors and assume that he held a certain air about himself because of his royal status. Never would Tiatana have imagined that her son would get to this point. Tears began to well in the former queen's eyes as it fully began to sink in exactly what her own flesh and blood was truly capable of.

"That was your last chance to be silent. Speak again, and the goblins will have you." Rowan walked away again and Tiatana could hear him rustling through Alston's desk.

"Sire?" a raspy voice spoke.

"Yes, what is it, Caul?" Rowan replied to his goblin henchman.

"The goblins have all arrived. They've gathered in the throne room. What order shall I give?"

"Have them venture into the kingdom and begin removing the nymphs from their homes. Lock anyone you capture in the dungeon underneath the palace. I need to locate a book of my father's that I haven't seen since I was younger, but I know is in here somewhere. He was given the book by Labete himself."

"What book is that, my liege?"

"The Forest's Book of the Dead."

CHAPTER 4

Garmon's small army marched their way to Nymph Kingdom, keeping a quickened pace to make good time. The group had traveled for quite a while, a long enough time for Felix to start to feel a tickling within his legs. He knew that if he continued on any further, he would surely lose the feeling in them altogether.

"All right," Garmon announced when they had reached a shady area underneath a bramble bush. "Let's rest here for a little while. I'll let you know when it's time to leave again. Don't," he said, staring directly from Felix to Eleonora, "wander off."

"Thank the Yew," Felix whispered to his faery friend as they sat down together. "I don't think I could have walked much further. My legs are killing me."

"Then why don't you ride on Basil?" Eleonora replied sweetly. "I'm sure he wouldn't mind."

Felix grimaced. "You know I can't allow Garmon the pleasure of witnessing that."

"Everybody needs some help sometimes, you know," Eleonora said, placing her hand on Felix's shoulder. "It's nothing to be ashamed of. Didn't your parents ask for help when they were ending the falling? From witches?"

"Yes, I suppose they did," Felix grumbled. "But I don't have to do things exactly how they did it."

"Of course not! It's just... well, I think that the only thing to really be ashamed of is pride. We are all on this earth to help each other anyway. Isn't that the point of life?"

"I guess I'm just not well-versed in the meaning of life yet," Felix replied. Eleonora rolled her eyes playfully and handed her nymph friend a good-sized slice of bread.

"Eat up," she said. "We don't want those legs going out on us, now, do we?"

"Eleonora!" Garmon called out. "Eleonora, I have some faery cake. Would you like to join me?"

Eleonora glanced at Felix, who hung his head as he munched on his bread. "Oh, um, thank you, Garmon, but I think I'm okay here. Enjoy the cake, though."

Garmon exhaled loudly, and fiddled with a thin, silver chain that dangled delicately from his neck. "As you wish, Eleonora," he said, and his voice suddenly grew louder and harsher. "Just a moment more, everybody! Finish up your snacks and prepare to leave!"

Garmon's voice reverberated loudly through the trees, and Felix began to notice that the Forest was eerily quieter than usual. He felt a sharp pang towards the back of his head, a brief twinge of a headache that only lasted for a brief moment, and yet was overly noticeable. He tried to chalk it up to his hunger, and perhaps his tired legs as well, so ultimately decided to ignore it, like he had earlier that day.

"Myso!" Basil called out, and the troll rushed over to his skunk friend.

"What is it, Basil?" Myso replied.

"I have something for you," the skunk said teasingly.

As Myso grew closer he noticed that Basil had found particularly chubby grub that was writhing around in a small dirt hole that the skunk had dug while searching for a quick snack. Myso leaned down, and studied the grub for a moment before turning to his friend.

"Is this for me to eat?" the troll asked.

"Yes, give it a good poke then it will be ready for consumption," Basil replied, with a hint of mischief in his voice and a twinkle in his eye. Myso could see that something was sneaky about the tone of his good friend's voice, but yet crept closer to the hole, then reached one of his round, stubby fingers down to the grub and gave it a good poke.

The grub wriggled, then suddenly squirted a putrid-smelling liquid up at the troll, covering his hand and part of his arm with the yellowish-white stench. Myso yelped, and jumped back while Basil rolled around on the ground, laughing uncontrollably. After frantically wiping the liquid off his hand and arm with a leaf, Myso turned to his friend and joined in his laughter.

"Something funny?" Garmon broke in, glaring at the skunk and troll.

"Sorry, Garmon!" Myso and Basil replied in unison.

"Break time is over," Garmon said curtly. "Everyone get up, and let's get moving. Myso, weren't you supposed to be keeping watch?"

"Yes, Garmon," the troll replied. "Terribly sorry. I'll go ahead and make sure our path is clear."

Myso had always been one to take heed of any legends or warnings that came with the Forest's history. He was well-versed in his studies, and made a point to keep himself updated on any new goings-on of the Forest. Though trolls were notorious for having short tempers—and Myso was certainly not innocent of that trait—he felt that awareness of his potential to explode only helped him further control it. He prided himself on being insightful, and trying to look at any given situation from every possible angle. But he also found that his need to exert pent-up aggression made him suited for being a warrior, and a very good one at that. He could fulfill his need to discover, learn, and ponder, yet also be provided with an outlet for his energy when provided the opportunity.

Myso darted out down the path the group was following, looking around in all directions and shifting the iridescence of his spiky hair from jet back to purple each time the sun shone upon his head from a different angle. Myso was tan, and fairly streamlined except for a slightly protruding belly. His ears were over-sized and sharply pointed, and his eyes were big, bright, and lavender in color. Myso continued to scan the scenery until he spotted some slight movement in the trees to his right, just ahead of the path that the army was following.

No being was discernible, only quick movements of the trees and strange flashes of light. After staring for a moment, Myso began to make out several orbs of grayish white light darting around amongst the trees. He noticed that Garmon was catching up with him, so he picked up a pebble nearby and gently tossed it in the faery's direction, leading him to focus his attention on the strange balls of light drifting around within the trees.

The orbs floated around in circles, and began to draw within the air visibly discernible shapes, outlines of humanoid figures gathered together in a group, crouched over to hide within the brush. As the shapes became clearer, it was apparent that the sighting was indeed one lost in time, a vision of what once was spanned over generations of the earth holding within it the energy of the past.

The figures solidified except for a slight misty quality surrounding them, and Myso could now see that he was viewing a long-forgotten hunt, one performed by the native humans when they used to inhabit the Forest. The native peoples had long since migrated out of the area, for reasons unknown to the current inhabitants, but clearly a residual energy of the emotional impact of the native people's disappearance was not forgotten by the land.

As Myso and Garmon stared longer, their silence prompted the other three members of the group to take notice of the spectacle once they caught up to them. All five beings stared in silence as the apparitions of the native humans stalked an invisible animal within the trees, attacking and slaughtering it violently. The ghostly animal, presumably a deer or other large creature, was dragged away from the group, fading off into the distance. Then suddenly, the entire manifestation disappeared completely.

"That was strange, wasn't it?" Eleonora whispered.

"What were those things? Ghosts?" Felix asked.

"I believe so. I think we just witnessed a manifestation of a past event in the Forest. Native humans have not resided in this part of the Forest for a very long time," Myso replied.

"But why would such a specter just randomly appear?" Eleonora inquired.

"That I do not know. But part of me feels like it has something to do with King Alston's recent demise," Myso said.

"Well, we shall be extra careful as we continue on, then," Garmon retorted confidently. "But I will not be intimidated by ghosts."

The pain in Felix's head now seemed to grow stronger, spreading across the entire width of his brain. He tried his hardest not to wince, but couldn't help the force of his eyes slamming shut and squeezing tightly over his eyeballs as the throbbing increased.

"Is something wrong, Felix?" Eleonora's voice pierced through his pain.

"I just have a headache, that's all," Felix replied nonchalantly. "I'll be fine, don't worry."

"Weakling," Garmon snickered, quietly enough so Felix shouldn't have been able to hear him. Oddly enough, through his headache he strangely felt as though his senses were somewhat intensified. Garmon's insult spoke loudly within his ears, but his headache was now so severe that he chose to ignore it.

Grandson of Ginia, a voice now boomed within the pounding of his mind. Nymph by name of Felix, nephew of Nyxen, son of Narena...

Felix grabbed his head, willing the voice to stop. He was not in any mood to deal with strange voices at this time, and didn't feel ready to accept what he now knew was happening to him. His uncle, Nyxen, as well as his grandmother, Ginia, were tree whisperers, and Felix was certain that this phenomenon was what was now afflicting him.

"No," he whispered as quietly as he could. "Not now, please!"

"What was that?" Eleonora broke in, and Felix felt her hand on his shoulder once again.

"Nothing," he hissed. "It's just a headache."

Felix continued to deny the pain within his thoughts, and found after a moment that the headache began to slowly subside, until he no longer felt the throbs nor pangs in his brain. He breathed a sigh of relief as he continued walking with the group, but still wondered why, of all times, this was now happening to him.

CHAPTER 5

The army continued on their journey to Nymph Kingdom, and soon passed the dwelling of the only humans known to presently reside within the Forest, the witches of the Elder Triage. Their tree home was a large log cabin with a dungeon-like front door and crescent moon-shaped peek hole situated by a towering old oak tree. It looked quite homey, except for one giant hole in the side of the house that looked as though it had been repaired at some point. Thick pieces of bark worn and covered with moss were patched onto the side of the home, leaving one side of the tree without a window.

In front of the tree home stood a tall, thin man with a long gray beard. He wore slacks and a button-up shirt, with a long olive-green cloak over his entire outfit. He appeared to merely be enjoying the sunshine of the day, humming to himself as he looked around at the flowers and buzzing insects at his feet. Upon hearing the small army approach, the man stood upright and squinted his eyes to see who it was that happened to be walking by.

"Shouldn't this house be invisible?" Felix hissed to Eleonora. "It was in all the stories my parents told me. You have to do a chant or a spell or something to make it appear."

"I don't know," Eleonora replied, her eyes fixed on the man. "Maybe they feel like they don't need to hide their home anymore. Because of the Forest's overall approval of the witches now."

"Hello there, little beings!" the man chuckled, breaking through Felix and Eleonora's conversation. "Where are you off to on this fine day?" The man gave a knowing smile, as if he were already aware of the purpose of their journey.

"Hello, sir. We are a multi-species army stationed out of Troll Kingdom. We are on our way to Nymph Kingdom. Good day!" Garmon replied curtly.

"And what is it you intend to do there?" the man asked with wide, sea-foam green eyes.

"I don't believe that is any of your business. I am following strict orders from my king," Garmon retorted, looking straight up at the man.

"Well, you certainly are a big personality for such a small being!"

"Good day, sir."

"Wait..."

"Really, sir, we must be on our way," Garmon said, starting to walk away, and motioned for the group to follow.

"I wouldn't go back there if I were you," the man said frankly, in a lower-pitched tone. Garmon stopped mid-step, sighed, and turned around.

"And why is that?"

"Well, first of all, Nymph Palace is overrun with goblins."

"WHAT?!" the entire group cried in unison.

"Afraid so."

"I knew that King Alston had perished, but that was all I was told!" Garmon practically yelled upwards at the tall man.

"It's more than that, little one. Why don't you come inside? I'll explain all of it to you."

"I'm afraid we cannot. We must report immediately. We're expected," Garmon said, panicking at the thought of being even a moment late. His reputation was on the line.

"As you wish. But if you find that you need anything more, I'll be here. I'm staying with the Elder Triage for awhile. My name is Magus, by the way."

"Hello, Magus. And thank you for your offer, but I don't think we will be needing anything else." Garmon began to scoot his army away.

"We'll see!" Magus replied in a sing-song voice.

Garmon rolled his eyes and walked on, glancing at the position of the sun.

"Why didn't we stay and speak with that wizard? I don't know about you, Garmon, but I certainly have no desire to walk right into a goblin ambush!" Felix ran to catch up with Garmon, who was briskly walking ahead. Eleonora fluttered behind the two, looking worried, and eavesdropping on the conversation.

"This is not for you to decide, Felix," Garmon snapped, quickening his pace and avoiding eye contact with the nymph.

"And it is your decision to march us straight to our doom?"

"We do not know that the wizard was not simply making things up! Wizards are very imaginative, you know."

"What reason would he have for fabricating a story solely for the purpose of frightening us? I strongly believe that was a warning!"

"Then take it as such! And prepare yourself mentally as if you were entering battle. You've trained for many years for such situations, you should well know what you're doing by now! And if you don't, well, that is for fate to decide."

"But you take the name of fate as if you have a right doing so! You'd better hope your spears soar fast enough to keep up with your mouth." Felix stormed away from Garmon.

In all his frustration, Felix found he was more out of breath than usual, so finally submitted to riding atop Basil's back. There, the nymph closed his eyes and tried to meditate to center himself, something he was taught to do at a very young age by a salamander friend of his mother's. He was thankful his headache was gone, even if it were now replaced with a new headache—dealing with Garmon.

This was certainly not the first time Felix and Garmon had butted heads. Their personal feuds with one another started long ago, back when Felix was first stationed in Troll Kingdom. Naturally, Felix took a liking to the pretty and bubbly Eleonora straight away, much to the dismay of Garmon, who had been trying to win her affections for quite a while prior to Felix's arrival. But Eleonora was never one to be swayed by a male's power or status, and tried her best to avoid contact with Garmon as much as possible, spending all of her free time building a foundation of friendship with Felix, whom she found to be not only strong and intelligent, but handsome and quite intriguing as well. Whether or not Garmon was aware of Eleonora's feelings towards him was debatable, but it was likely in all his pride he was ignorant to the fact that Eleonora harbored romantic feelings for anyone besides himself, so continued to pursue her time and time again.

Garmon's ambivalence and hostility toward Felix did not only stem from the nymph's feelings for Eleonora, however. Garmon felt intimidated by Felix from the moment he met him. He was, after all, the son of Narena and Kellen, saviors of the Forest, and true warriors in their own right, despite Narena never having actually been trained as one. And Felix was also the grandson of Felide, General of the Nymph Army under King Alston's rule. All signs pointed to Felix becoming as accomplished as his family, and that thought conflicted with Garmon's own personal goal of becoming a general. So Garmon always tried to make an example of Felix, using his superior ranking to humiliate him whenever possible, ensuring that any witnesses—especially Eleonora—would see that the nymph wasn't receiving special treatment solely based on his blood. Eleonora never seemed to take notice of Felix's faults the way Garmon did, but Garmon was determined to continue to try to prove his point.

The group made sure to stay as quiet as possible as they walked for quite some time, and finally crossed the threshold into Nymph Kingdom. Felix disembarked from Basil's back and walked on his own, crouching and ducking around various rocks, branches, and leaves. Garmon stayed at the front of the group, using hand signals to indicate to them when to move to a closer position. Myso stayed towards the back, watching behind them to ensure that no one was creeping up on them undetected. When they began to pass by Felix's parents' humble home within the hollows of an oak tree—the very house in which Narena and her brother, Nyxen, once resided together—Felix ran to the door and motioned at the group to go inside; which they did, much to the surprise of Felix's parents who were sitting at a table in the kitchen.

"Well, look who it is!" Kellen said happily, getting up to embrace his son. His wife, Narena, did the same, and the rest of the army stood awkwardly in the foyer of the home.

"Felix Hawthorne!" Narena cried out with glee, then suddenly smacked herself on the head. "Drat! I forgot that I wanted to lock that door. Not to keep you out, Felix, of course, but my seer sight has really been acting up today. Something is brewing about the Forest, I'm sure of it."

"Yes, my dear, you've been saying that," Kellen said softly while playfully rolling his eyes.

"Well, it's nice to see you, Mother. And Father," Felix beamed at his parents as he turned his body slightly to lock the door behind the army.

Though they had lived happily for many years since their own harrowing ordeal during the time of the falling, Narena and Kellen didn't look as though they had aged a day since, aside from a few gray hairs that wove into their dark-colored locks.

Kellen was muscular and tall with soft green eyes, and blessed with striking good looks and dark features. His wife, Narena, was small for a nymph, with sparkling orange eyes and wavy, messy hair. She was adorable—quite lovely, actually—yet was so concerned with matters of the mind that she was beyond acknowledging her beauty, even after years of her husband pointing it out to her daily. Narena had always felt that if someone in the relationship deserved recognition for good looks, it would be Kellen, and preferred to refer to herself as the thinker of the two. Which was fine with Kellen, as he was a proficient warrior in his own right, and always eager and willing to support his wife in any and all of her morally-backed sentiments.

"Now, what brings our darling son back to us today?" Narena said, prompting a sarcastic chuckle out of Garmon. Narena shot him a piercing, orange-eyed glare then turned back to her son.

"Wait, you don't know? King Alston is dead, Mother. And... well, we ran into a wizard on our way here. He says the palace is overrun with goblins."

"Goblins?! Oh my, that is indeed a problem. See, Kellen? I told you!" Narena smacked Kellen's bicep. "Now, Felix, how did this happen?" Her eyes perked with interest.

"I have no idea. All I know is that Alston is dead, and we were sent back to handle the situation. How could you not have been informed of this?"

"Well, my son, I'd imagine that if the palace is completely taken over, we wouldn't have been told about it. We haven't needed to report to the palace in the last few days," Kellen replied.

Felix found himself surprised at how blasé his parents seemed to be about the whole situation. Were they not aware of the magnitude of what was going on? Or perhaps in all their own adventures, they had seen and experienced so much that they no longer harbored fear for the unknown. Felix could only assume that sentiment, and only further admire his parents for how calm and collected they were under pressure.

"Where's Grandfather?" Felix asked, furrowing his brow.

"He hasn't been around for weeks," Kellen replied. "King Alston sent him on a mission to some faraway land. I doubt he'll be back anytime soon."

"Do you know what the mission was?"

"That I don't. He said it was top secret, and he wouldn't return for months. It would be nice to have him around, if what you say is happening is indeed true."

Kellen squinted his eyes slightly at his son, as if gauging his response to his statement. But Felix was well-versed in his father's attempts to dig reactions out of him, especially in regards to Felide, so maintained an expression that was dull as a stone.

"Excuse me, I hate to break up the family reunion here, but we are under strict orders to report to the palace immediately!" Garmon interrupted the family's conversation.

"Oh, pardon me. What is your name, sir?" Narena asked, looking slightly offended by the faery's interruption.

"Garmon. I am leader of the multi-species army in Troll Kingdom. I hold the title of best spear warrior in the land," Garmon said, looking proud of himself.

"Wow, in the whole land? That's pretty impressive," Kellen said mockingly. Felix tried to hide his smile.

"Yes. You should know better than anyone of the importance to report in a timely manner. We need to stop these goblins before their numbers increase and they start venturing into the kingdom, and maybe even come knocking on your door!"

"Well, Garmon, Narena and I are well-prepared for such an event. Have you not heard of our own accomplishments?" Kellen replied calmly.

"Indeed I have, and I owe you my gratitude for what you have done for the Forest. But..."

"Where did you see the wizard?" Narena interrupted with a curious smile.

"Um, outside of the witches' tree home."

"The Elder Triage home?" Narena asked with bright eyes, and she grabbed Kellen's hand and squeezed it.

"Yes."

"What are all of your names?" Narena asked, scanning each member of the group before focusing her glance at Basil. She smiled at him. He looked around awkwardly then smiled back.

"This is Eleonora, faery bow warrior," Felix said before Garmon could jump in. The faery looked annoyed. "The troll here is Myso, a spear and blade warrior. And our skunk is named Basil. You can only imagine what kind of warrior he is!"

"Hello, everyone. I'm Narena, and this is Kellen," the female nymph beamed.

"We know who you are! Wow, what an honor this is, indeed!" Eleonora replied quickly, and rushed over to Narena to shake her hand.

Narena looked over the female faery for a moment with a curious smile, and upon deciding that she seemed to be quite a nice faery, held out her hand in return, pulling Eleonora into a warm, motherly embrace.

"Mother, I know you do not fear what lies in the palace, but I really have to urge you and Father to leave Nymph Kingdom at once. I have no doubts you are a worthy opponents for the goblins, but out of love for me, I beg of you, flee this area," Felix said, placing his hand on his mother's shoulder as she hugged his friend.

"Yes, do allow us to perform our duties, please," Garmon said under his breath.

"Have you all forgotten that we are all under protection of the Higher Spirits?" Narena broke in.

"And that our Higher Spirit of protection has been destroyed?" Garmon continued in a grumpy tone. "By the very nymphs who stand before us, might I add."

"Well, technically Agrimon destroyed Labete. We just destroyed the negative fusion of the two. Get it right, buddy," Kellen snapped.

"I'm not your buddy! I'm not even your son's buddy! I am the leader of this army, and I order all members to stand down, lest you face my wrath! Trust me, you would rather face Gorgon himself than deal with me when I'm angry!" Garmon practically yelled.

"When *aren't* you angry, Garmon?" Felix broke in, visibly upset. "How dare you speak to my parents this way. I would never be this disrespectful to any member of your family."

"Say one more word, Felix, and I will hold you in contempt for the remainder of this mission!" Garmon got right up in Felix's face.

"What is that supposed to mean? You won't slow down your fluttery pace for me anymore? Boo-hoo!"

"Why, I ought to..."

Knock, knock, knock.

"Someone's at the door!" Kellen hissed. "Everybody stay back, I'll handle this. It's probably one of our neighbors."

"I doubt it," Garmon muttered.

Kellen went to the door and looked through the small peek hole with Narena directly behind him, pressing her body up against his back on the tips of her toes to peer around his shoulder. Much to their surprise and horror, they found themselves looking straight into muddy, piercing gray eyes. Kellen fumbled with the latch to ensure it was indeed locked before the knob began to turn on its own. It jiggled slightly, then began to shake around violently. Whoever was on the other side of the door furiously banged upon it, and a voice echoed into the house.

"Open this door this instant, by order of the king!" a raspy voice screamed through the door.

Garmon signaled for the warriors to pull out their weapons, and readied his own spear. Kellen pushed Narena behind a sitting chair in the living room and grabbed his bow and arrow, which were hanging on a rack near the front door. Narena rolled her eyes at her overprotective husband, grabbed a long blade she had hidden under the chair, and rushed out to join the others.

"By way of what king?" Kellen shouted confidently through the door.

Whatever was outside was quiet for a moment, and Kellen peeked through the hole to find the gray eyes were still indeed present, but looking as though they were deep in thought.

"Is it still there?" Eleonora whimpered.

"Yes," Kellen hissed. "Be ready to fight, everyone. It looks like a goblin to me."

"By way of the king who rightly wears the crown! Son of Alston. The rightful heir to the throne!" the raspy voice hissed through the door. Felix uncontrollably shivered, and felt a momentary pang radiate through his head.

"Alston's son is dead. He has been so for a long time," Kellen replied to the voice.

"Of course he is!" the voice replied, and eerie silence ensued for a brief moment.

Suddenly, the front door came crashing through the foyer into the living room, causing Kellen to leap backwards and the entire group to disperse throughout the front room and foyer. A huge, thick tree branch came sliding into the room just narrowly missing Felix as he rushed to grab his mother and Eleonora, pulling the two females into the kitchen with him.

Dust filled the room, causing everyone to cough and strain their eyes to see what lay within it. The warriors readied their weapons as the dust began to settle, but before anyone could get a good view of what had entered, several goblins ran into the house with long, jagged spears. They rounded everyone up, disarmed them, and surrounded them in a circle, spears pointed directly at their hearts. Caul, Rowan's henchman, entered last, and looked around at all the beings, laughing maniacally at them as he heaved hot breath and drool in their faces.

The goblins outweighed the nymphs and faeries, though they were only slightly taller than a troll, and carried themselves in a menacing way that caused them to appear much bigger than they actually were. They were nearly rail-thin, and their spinal columns curved upwards and down from their backs like a question mark, making them appear as if they were always looming over their prey, like a vulture guarding its carrion. They had wide heads, sharp, jagged teeth, and long, thin tongues that lapped around in their rotting mouths as they hissed at their potential victims.

Goblins did not reside in any defined kingdom—they mainly kept to the unincorporated outskirts of the Forest in small numbers, as they were banned from having a kingdom of their own long ago by the Higher Spirits in an attempt to lessen their population. Goblins lived for chaos— they worshiped Gorgon blindly, and were trained in their dastardly deeds by Doppel, whom they also inherited their deceptive nature.

Throughout the Forest's history, goblins had been known for exacerbating negative situations, and helping those throughout time who had been dead set on destruction of the Forest and its kingdoms. Merely witnessing a goblin within the confines of the kingdoms protected by the Higher Spirits was a bad omen in itself.

Caul led his goblin followers out of Kellen and Narena's home, dragging the group along with them in the direction of the palace. As they walked, Felix peeked around his captors and noticed that there were goblins everywhere, breaking down doors of homes and dragging the nymph inhabitants out into the open. Felix could not see where the other nymphs were being taken, but he could only assume that it was a fate similar to his current predicament.

Once the goblins had successfully shoved the group into the palace, Caul demanded that they bring the group to see Rowan immediately in the throne room. They entered the room and saw Rowan, crown upon his head, sitting delicately on the throne, gaunt and grotesque as ever. He raised his sunken eyes to look upon the group as they approached, and cackled as the goblins shoved the beings to the ground to bow before him. Narena and Kellen covered their heads with their arms.

"Here is the strange group we captured, my liege. They must be warriors; why else would two faeries, a troll, and a skunk be in Nymph Kingdom?" Caul hissed at Rowan, keeping his gray eyes to the ground.

"This is a strange group indeed. But wait—what is this?" the rotting nymph king inquired.

Rowan stepped down from the throne and began to pace around the circle of beings. He stopped directly in front of Narena and Kellen and stared down at them.

"Don't look at him," Narena whispered. "He's emerged from the underworld. His eyes can influence."

"I saw him already, and trust me, you don't want to see what he's become anyway," Kellen hissed jokingly in reply.

"What was that, Kellen?" Rowan sneered.

"Hello, old friend. It's been a long time," Kellen in a strangely jovial tone, peering up but not looking directly at Rowan's wretched, rotting face. If he was fearful of Rowan's intentions he wasn't showing it in the slightest.

"Ah yes. Friend. A real good friend you are, to leave a fallen warrior behind."

"Rowan, we were all running away. I didn't even see you fall. I didn't know you had, or else I would have helped you."

"I should kill you right now, just like my father. I swore to Gorgon that I would destroy all those who failed me, and you are certainly no exception. But I won't, just yet. I want you to see your precious Forest suffer for awhile first."

"I didn't mean to fail you, Rowan. We were friends. I cared for you deeply."

"You didn't know, my father didn't know, even the Higher Spirits did nothing to save my soul. Only the Under Spirits were willing to help me. 'Tis a pity they have such a horrible reputation. Let's see your Higher Spirits help you out of this one." Rowan turned his attention to Caul. "Throw Kellen and Narena in the dungeon with the other prisoners you've collected around the kingdom. Toss the others in my quarters with my mother. I still have some questions for them, and I don't want their responses tainted by these two meddling nymphs. But first, I need to finalize the opening of the doorway."

Felix and Eleonora exchanged glances, then Felix looked at his parents, who were mouthing to each other that they were unaware that Nymph Palace even had a dungeon. Which was odd, given the fact that both Narena and Kellen practically spent their whole childhood and adolescent lives residing in the palace. But though King Alston was certainly one who was keen on flaunting his wealth and status, advertising the fact that his palace contained a dungeon was not something he was apt to do. The king kept to himself, at the palace, rarely leaving unless he absolutely had to, and stayed out of inter-Forest affairs. Alston having a dungeon was not something out of the realm of possibilities, especially given his view toward helping others and overall stern demeanor.

Felix remembered that his father once referred to Alston as a 'weak king', and that once the falling had ended and his parents were palace advisers, Alston still kept some of his old ways despite his claim that he was turning over a new leaf. The more Felix thought about everything he knew about the royal family, the more he ascertained that Alston was a man of many secrets. The unspoken dungeon was probably just the start of it.

"Yes, my liege," Caul hissed in reply to Rowan's command, and the goblins hurried to remove all the captive beings from Rowan's sight. Felix watched as his mother and father were dragged away, as he and his army were led into the king's quarters and shoved inside, with the door violently slamming and locking behind them.

CHAPTER 6

Felix rushed to Eleonora once he heard the goblins walk away from the door of the king's quarters. He embraced her, holding her tightly, and felt the wetness of her tears soak into the shoulder of his tunic. Myso and Basil stood aside, but the troll reached over to pat the faery's back. Garmon began wandering about the room and came upon a lovely older female nymph tied to a chair by the window with a handkerchief stuffed in her mouth. He rushed over and removed it, quickly untying her.

"Are you all right, ma'am? I'm Garmon, leader of this multi-species army. You are under our full protection now, do not fear!"

"And how do you intend to protect her when we cannot even protect ourselves?" Felix let go of Eleonora and walked over to the chair. Garmon ignored the nymph and kept his eyes locked on the lovely older female, a smile creeping over his normally grumpy face.

"I'm quite all right, I must assure you. Thank you, Garmon. I'm Tiatana, Queen of Nymph Kingdom. Well, former Queen of Nymph Kingdom, I suppose now."

"This is my army—Eleonora, Myso, Basil, and Felix. I'm Garmon," the male faery beamed, his eyes fixed unwaveringly upon the queen.

"Yes, you said that," Tiatana replied, looking a bit uncomfortable, and yet relieved at the same time.

Felix rolled his eyes. "You'd think he'd never seen a beautiful nymph before," he whispered to Eleonora, who giggled. Garmon inhaled and exhaled loudly, yet refused to acknowledge Felix's comment.

Felix, Eleonora, Myso, and Basil gathered around the queen, introducing themselves to her even as their eyes still darted around the room in panic. Basil began to wander about, sniffing around the rug and under the furniture.

The king's quarters was a large room in which one wall consisted entirely of a bookcase nearly spilling over with books, papers, and various statues and trinkets. In front of it, stood a desk, also cluttered with papers and books opened to random pages. In the center of the room was a long table with what looked like a three dimensional map of the Forest. It was now smashed through the center, and pieces were torn off and scattered about the floor. An enormous window took up another wall of the room, with the sitting chair positioned to look out onto the kingdom, so Alston was able to survey his land in the utmost comfort. It was there now presumably so Tiatana could witness firsthand the extent of destruction upon her kingdom.

Myso sat down, cross-legged, in front of the window, and watched as goblins continued to break into homes and drag screaming nymphs from the interiors. The troll closed his eyes and began to speak a quiet protection incantation to himself, rocking back and forth on his legs and trying his best to concentrate despite all the sadness and havoc before him. He prayed to Sator, asking for direction in their plight, but found in his frustration at his imprisonment that he was distracted. Basil sat down next to him and curled up at his side, closing his black skunk eyes and trying to provide support to his good friend.

The door suddenly swung open and Caul entered the room, baring his teeth at the beings as he walked over to the window where the chair was. Two goblin henchmen stood in the doorway, blocking the beings' only exit.

"You!" Caul sneered, pointing at the queen. "You're coming with us." He writhed across the room and grabbed her by the wrist, leading her towards the door.

"Where are you taking her?" Garmon stood up and shouted at him.

"None of your business, Faery," Caul snapped back as he scooted the queen out of the room. Tiatana cocked her head back, and was able to mouth a message to Garmon just before the door slammed in his face.

"What did she say to you?" Eleonora asked, wiping residual tears from her eyes and smearing tear marks across her cheeks, matting her thick eyelashes.

"She said, 'the bookcase'," Garmon replied. He walked around the desk and stared up at the towering wall of shelves.

"What about the bookcase?" Felix chimed in.

"I don't know. That's all she said," Garmon snapped back.

"Is there something we should find in the bookcase?" Eleonora asked.

She walked over to Garmon and stood next to him, scanning the rows of books that were shoved haphazardly throughout the shelves. Garmon turned to her and discreetly wrapped his arm around her waist as the two perused the bookcase, not entirely sure what it was they were actually looking for. Felix noticed and walked over, hopelessly looking around at the mess before him. He watched the two faeries out of the corner of his eye, not wanting to upset Eleonora more than she already was by confronting Garmon's inappropriateness, and trying to ignore the anger that was now boiling over at the sight he was now witnessing.

Felix had tried many times throughout his friendship with Eleonora to express his feelings for her, but fear of rejection or the possibility that she simply wouldn't be interested based on his species always prevented him from doing so. He had always tried to play it off as if they were good friends, but his attentiveness to her revealed his true feelings to those who were interested enough to observe their interactions. Garmon was one of those—he was probably the only being who ever made an effort to do so—and Felix cringed as he thought of the fact that Garmon had always made it his own personal mission to do anything and everything to get in his way.

But to Felix, Eleonora was well worth any inconvenience that Garmon could throw at him. She was stunning physically, and endearing, and not just in the way that faeries intrigue with the way they sparkle as they flutter about. She had an inherent beauty about her that can only truly be understood by someone who knew her well, like in the way Felix did. Her eyes and hair glimmered with any light that caught their glare, and her spunky personality always seemed to keep Felix guessing. True, she wasn't the smartest faery nor was she the most skilled warrior, but Eleonora provided an unspoken comfort to Felix that he had only known in one other female—his mother. And though there were no other similarities between the two, the comfort that Eleonora provided was a close enough resemblance for him.

Felix wondered if his parents felt the panic and anxiety that came along with not having one bit of control over the given situation. He assumed that they would be well-versed in the trials and tribulations that comes with combating evil, but his protectiveness over his family overrode any sense of feeling like they had their situation under control.

In the past, they had the advantage of walking freely through the Forest along their journey to defeat Labete, but now what were they to do, locked in a dungeon, with no possible way out and no allies left who were not yet already captured?

Felix couldn't shake the thoughts of a possible harrowing outcome for the nymphs who gave him life. He knew that if he could persevere through his own ordeal in the king's quarters, his next task would be attempting to free those locked away downstairs. That is, if Garmon didn't get in the way.

Garmon was never one to follow anyone's rules but his own. Sometimes not even his own, as he was prone to changing his mind or feelings about a situation or problem at any given time. It was all dependent on how he was feeling that particular day, or who may have bestowed upon him the most beneficial outcome for himself.

Well at least there was one constant, Felix thought. Garmon generally sided with whatever would make Eleonora happy, so Felix resolved himself to the thought that he and Garmon had at least one thing in common.

"So, Eleonora, would you have ever possibly imagined that we would be in such a predicament?" Garmon asked, seemingly unfazed by the position he was currently in.

"Um, well, no, I suppose not. But I did anticipate such excitement, as I am a warrior, after all," Eleonora replied, raising an eyebrow at the faery.

"And a very fine one at that! My dear, there is indeed greatness ahead of you. I can feel it," Garmon gushed. Felix had to stop himself from rolling his eyes at Garmon's groveling.

"Thank you, Garmon. That's very kind of you to say."

"Oh, come on," Felix groaned. "Just not one moment ago you were stumbling over your words in the presence of Tiatana! And to think, I assumed you would never fall for the feminine wiles of a *nymph*!"

"Shut your mouth, dirt-walker," Garmon snapped. "I can appreciate beauty on any being, regardless of species or age. And furthermore, don't you think the Queen deserves some comfort after losing her husband? How heartless of you."

"I'm heartless? You are certainly one to talk! Now I've seen your true colors, Garmon. You'd gladly pursue any female so long as she perks your interest in the moment! Why don't you go save the Queen and leave the rest of us to worry about the kingdoms?"

"You'd like that, wouldn't you, Felix? Well how about this—I intend on staying just to irritate you!" Garmon turned to Eleonora, and his demeanor quickly softened. "I'm so happy that the fates have inspired us to have this journey together, Eleonora, and I know that it is because of our mutual respect and love for one another that our army will succeed."

Garmon subconsciously twiddled with the amulet around his neck, waiting for Eleonora to reply. But she did not, and instead continued looking around in front of her, looking somewhat annoyed.

Felix pulled over the desk chair, climbing on it and standing as tall as he could. He thought for a moment, and closed his eyes. Then the headache came back with a vengeance, and Felix had to grab hold of the chair to keep his balance.

"Not again," he groaned to himself. Then the voice spoke.

Felix... Felix...

"What? What is it?" Felix said aloud.

"What's going on?" Eleonora asked, but Felix was too overwhelmed to notice.

Felix, the row of dusty books just above your head. Look behind them.

"Might as well, right?" Felix mumbled, opening his eyes and seeing the books the voice was speaking of. He knocked the entire row off the shelf with one swipe of his arm, crashing the books to the floor loudly and drawing the entire group's attention to him.

"Quiet down, would you? The goblins will hear!" Garmon scolded. Felix ignored him and stood as high on his toes as he could to get a better look at the empty shelf. Much to his excitement, he found that in the very back center of the shelf, was a small, rectangular door with a cherry wood spherical doorknob.

"Hey, look what I found!" Felix cried out. Garmon and Eleonora rushed over, with Myso and Basil behind them.

"What is it?" Eleonora asked.

"It's a little door of some kind," Felix replied.

"Well, let's open it!" Garmon announced.

"Wait, but it's much too small for any of us to fit through. It can barely fit an insect!" Felix exclaimed.

Garmon sighed, reaching his hand to the doorknob and turning it. The tiny door opened and revealed four wooden buttons attached to springs. Each button had a different picture etched onto the face, with a deer, a crow, a salamander, and a fish.

"The symbols..." Felix said quietly.

"What do they mean?" Eleonora asked, and stood right next to Felix with her shoulder leaning onto his.

"Well, they look to me as though they represent the four elements of the Forest. The deer is earth, the crow would be air, the salamander is fire, and the fish would be water," Felix replied confidently. He squared his shoulders and stood proudly upright, pleased that all the years of teachings from his mother on various matters of the Forest had finally paid off.

"Which button do we press?" Garmon asked, his voice sounding exasperated but still with a hint of curiosity.

"That, I do not know. What do you think, Myso?" Felix turned to the troll, who had been silently observing behind him.

"I've heard of these before. But I assumed that since there was a period of harmony prior to the falling, they no longer existed. If I'm correct in what this is, it's called an Elemeportal, and it's fueled by ancient magic of the Higher Spirits. Press a button, and you are subsequently sent to the realm of the element to which the picture on the button provides. It's a way out of here, certainly, but I can't say for sure where we'd be sent."

"So, we basically would jump locations?" Eleonora asked with wide eyes.

"In a sense, I believe so," Myso said, looking around at his comrades. The rest of the group looked frightened, yet slightly intrigued.

"Would we all be sent to another place, or would only the person who presses the button?" Garmon asked.

"I do not know. I've only heard of these, mind you, I've never actually seen one. In fact, I was under the impression that these were outlawed long ago in our Forest, so there's no guarantee that if we jump locations, we would be able to return as quickly as we arrived. If the area didn't have an Elemeportal, we'd have to find another way back, and who knows how long that could take!"

"The question is, then, are we willing to take that risk solely for the purpose of getting out of this room?" Felix said.

"Well, we could always split up, and some of us stay here while the others travel to an elemental realm," Garmon suggested, and Felix turned his head to roll his eyes.

"Of course you'd say that. Let me guess who you'd pick for your team," Felix mocked. "This isn't some game of Acornball, and we're not ten years old anymore. We are an army, and I'd think of all beings you'd realize that."

"How dare you speak to me that way! I make the decisions here, and I'm pulling rank!" Garmon nearly shouted.

"You think that your rank merits you to make such a decision?" Felix retorted. "I don't know about you, but I was taught in warrior training to stick with your group and leave no one behind. Sound familiar?"

"Stop it, you two," Myso interjected. "The goblins will hear you! How about this, I'll press..."

Myso was interrupted by the door swinging open once more, and Caul stood, hunched over the in the doorway, casting a bleak but menacing shadow into the room. Behind him, stood two goblin henchmen, holding long, jagged spears.

"What are they doing? *Get them!*" Caul shrieked, and the three goblins took off toward the bookcase, spears aimed straight on the little beings.

Felix had no time to think, so panicked, grabbing Eleonora and slamming his finger on one of the buttons while looking directly in the eyes of Caul. Whichever one was pressed, he did not see, but he squeezed his eyes shut and accepted his fate, as he began to feel a swirling sensation around his body.

Wherever we're going, Felix thought as he fully succumbed to the weightlessness of his body, *it has to be better than here.*

Felix felt a pit in his stomach, as though he had been twirling around in circles for hours without stopping. His body was now flying, but with no control. He opened his eyes to see his hand still clutching Eleonora's, and to his shock noticed, as he swirled through a vortex of colors and shooting lights, that Garmon was clutching onto Eleonora's other hand, floating through the Elemeportal with the two.

He must have grabbed on right as I pressed the button, Felix assumed. Though he was irritated that Garmon was with them, the portal seemed to gradually absolve him of all negative thoughts. And after all, having three minds on his side would ultimately be better than two.

Chapter 7

Caul and the goblin henchmen stood in awe, shocked and angered by the disappearance of the nymph and two faeries into thin air.

"Grab the troll and the skunk!" Caul shrieked at his henchmen, who instantaneously obliged. The goblins dragged Myso and Basil to the throne room and tossed them onto the ground in front of the throne, where Rowan sat with an old, tattered book opened in his lap.

"Why would you disturb my concentration, Caul?" Rowan sneered.

"My deepest apologies, sire, but I'm afraid I have some bad news," Caul replied.

"And what is that?" Rowan squinted his eyes at his henchman, and if looks could kill this certainly was one to accomplish just that.

"The nymph and two faeries... um... seem to have vanished. Into thin air."

"*What?!*" Rowan howled, bursting up from the throne. He stormed over to Caul and got right up in his face. His sunken eyes glowed red and unfocused, and he shot his arms forward, grasping Caul's neck tightly and squeezing harder every time the goblin flinched.

"Well, um, not really into thin air, my liege. Into the bookcase."

"The bookcase?! How in Gorgon's name does one disappear into a bookcase?!"

"I am sorry!" Caul choked. "We tried to grab them! We did manage to catch the troll and skunk, though!"

"Two out of five?" Rowan groaned. "You goblins are worthless. Now what am I to do? Those three were warriors! One was even the son of Kellen and Narena! How am I to please Doppel and deceive this Forest into a full-on haunting when three of my biggest adversaries are just walking freely about?"

"We can stop them, sire. It looked like there might have been a portal of some kind in the bookcase. We can go through the portal and follow them."

"And deny me your service? No, no, no, that won't work at all. They have to come back some time—we have the rest of their friends. There's no way those pathetic beings of light would allow their loved ones to perish without even an attempt at rescuing them. No, Caul, we will wait. Wait, like the ambush predators of the Forest, like a kalpie along the water's edge. Wait for them to return to the Forest, where I will have some nightmares awaiting their arrival. In the meantime, lock these ugly creatures away in the dungeon with the others, and do not let them escape. If they do, Caul, expect your fate to be worse than theirs. And bring my mother in here once you've finished with them. I have a bone to pick with her."

Caul nodded and grabbed Myso by the arm, digging his long, twisted fingernails into his flesh. Myso cried out in agony but choked back his sobs and glanced at Basil, who was being dragged out of the throne room by the remaining goblin henchman. Basil returned his glance with a helpless sigh, and the troll noticed that the skunk accidentally squirted out some of his musk in his uncontrollable terror. The goblin who was leading him cried out and stabbed the skunk in the back with his spear, drawing blood and prompting the skunk to release another squirt.

"He can't control it! Stop hurting him and he'll stop!" Myso cried out, causing Caul to jab him with his spear. The troll wailed in pain.

"Then every time he does it I'll make sure that you suffer the punishment," the goblin replied.

The troll and skunk were shoved through a hallway to a dead end, where Caul tugged on the arm of a statue of Alston and the wall in front of them opened to a staircase descending into darkness.

Felix slammed onto the wet ground. He scrambled to his feet, brushing off his tunic. The fabric was saturated with a thick, coarse, dirt-like material, yellowish-beige in color. It stuck to every part of him imaginable.

What is this strange stuff? he thought to himself. Then he heard Eleonora cough so he didn't dwell on it, focusing instead on locating the faery. He found her a couple of fox tail's lengths away and rushed over as quickly as he could. All around him, he could hear a faint roaring sound, disembodied but echoing across the scenery.

Eleonora sat up, and Felix knelt to embrace her on the ground, asking her if she was all right and rubbing her back. The faery nodded and coughed once more, picking up some of the material from the ground.

"What is this?" she asked, rubbing the thick dirt between her fingers.

"I don't know," Felix replied softly. "I was hoping you knew."

"It's sand, of course!" Garmon's voice floated over a mound of the material just behind where the two sat.

Felix and Eleonora stood up, and looked over the mound to find Garmon sitting in trickling stream of greenish-blue water. Felix bounded over the mound and helped the faery get on his feet.

"Sand? If there's sand, then we must be..." Felix trailed off.

"That's right. Turn around, would you?" Garmon said.

Felix turned his body to witness a massive amount of aquamarine water charging towards him, smashing into the ground and trailing moisture to his feet, then instantaneously pulling backwards, sucking the moisture away from the depths of the sand.

"Oh my Yew," Eleonora whispered.

"We're on a beach. We're at the coast. I've... never been this far from home," Felix said quietly.

Though he had always been hopeful of the promise of adventure, and chose by his own will to be stationed away from his kind in Troll Kingdom, Felix was a nymph who relished in his comforts—as most nymphs did, in fact. Never before had he been in a situation where he didn't inherently know his way home, though he had secretly wished for adventures to rival the ones his parents had had long ago. Felix was just simply not aware of how strong the thoughts of a being can manifest one's true desires up until this very moment.

"Well, if we're on the coast, my guess is that it would take up to two days to return to our Forest, and another half day just to arrive in Nymph Kingdom. And once we're back, then we have to deal with the goblins and Rowan," Garmon said, twiddling with his necklace as he spoke.

Felix was slightly surprised by how blasé Garmon was acting given their current predicament, but if Garmon was behaving calmly about a potentially harrowing experience, then Felix certainly should as well.

"Well, I guess we had better start moving, if we hope to make good time," Felix said.

This was the first time Felix had ever entertained the idea of submitting to Garmon's constant time constraints. But he knew that if he had any hope of rescuing his parents and friends, he would need to temporarily put aside his reluctance to befriend the male faery. They would need to work together this time, whether the two liked it or not.

"Let's walk parallel to the ocean," Garmon instructed. "We should eventually see a ridge or cliff side. Once we find that, we will need to figure out a way up, and we should be able to find the Forest from there. I remember that from my warrior studies—you two should have, also."

Felix and Eleonora looked around awkwardly and grumbled that they remembered, even though they exchanged glances conveying that they certainly hadn't.

So the three began walking, with Eleonora and Garmon squeezing the moisture out of their wings as they traveled. Their feet squished in the wet sand, causing them to sink slightly and leave tiny little footprints that faded away with the waves as they walked.

Suddenly, the three heard a raucous splashing that sounded as though it were fairly close. They squinted at the horizon to see if they could make out where the sound was coming from, but sunlight blocked their vision.

"Hello! Faeries! Over here!"

The voice sounded female, but seemed to be coming from nowhere. Finally, a mass of reddish-brown hair poked above a wave crashing close to where the beings stood. Garmon shoved Felix and Eleonora behind him and stood with his feet in the water.

"What do you want, water-being? We are on a mission!" Garmon shouted to the floating head, which giggled in return and submerged itself once more. The mass of hair popped up again, this time, in the shallower water closer to Garmon.

"Please tell me, because I am so curious as to this. Why on earth would you tiny little beings be all the way over here by my ocean? There are fish that hunt around here that could swallow all three of you in one gulp!"

The reddish-brown hair surrounded two big, cerulean blue eyes, a tiny button nose, and plump, red lips. The water-dwelling being herself was very fair, but she was only visible from the shoulders up.

"What do you want from us?" Garmon repeated curtly. "We are not here by our own accord."

"Well, it is you who should be wanting something from me. You look like you need help," the red-headed being replied with a grin.

Garmon sighed exasperatedly. "We do not need your help, miss."

"Well, are you at all interested in knowing which way to your Forest? Because if you would, I would strongly encourage you to turn your little bodies around and walk in the opposite direction."

The female being smiled a slightly crooked grin, and mischief danced around in her sparkling eyes. Garmon smacked himself on the head and turned around, storming off in the other direction. Felix and Eleonora looked slyly yet inquisitively at the mischievous water-being, and Felix kept the faery behind him as he approached the water.

"I desire to properly express my gratitude but I do not know your name nor what kind of species you are, miss," Felix's voice sounded a little shaky. He hoped that the female being didn't harbor any ideas of attempting to drown him if he moved any closer.

"You do not know of my species? You little beings truly are sheltered, that's for sure. I am an undine, of course! Tell me you have heard of us?" The undine giggled and her mane of hair shook around, despite it being nearly soaked to the bone.

"An undine? You mean a mermaid?" Eleonora asked, her eyes wide with excitement.

"I suppose some beings call us that. We prefer *undine*, just as you would prefer me call you a *faery* instead of a *buzzing insect*."

"But those aren't the same thing..." Eleonora said, her voice trailing off in confusion.

The undine laughed and flicked her tail up in the air. It glittered with iridescent scales of varying depths of green, catching every ray of sunlight that shone down from the sky.

"Exactly. Now what are your names?"

"I am Felix. This is Eleonora."

"And the grumpy one?"

"He's Garmon. We are all warriors stationed in Troll Kingdom."

"Trolls? Ew, I heard they smell terrible."

"I assure you they do not. Now what is your name, Undine?"

"My name is Sirenia."

"Nice to meet you, Sirenia. But I'm afraid we must be on our way—we already seem to have lost Garmon." Felix looked around but the male faery was nowhere in sight.

"Don't worry, you'll catch up to him. It's not like he can get very far."

"Wait, why is that, Sirenia?" Felix felt his stomach drop.

"Because you are on an island, of course!"

The undine giggled in a high-pitched tone, then submerged herself underwater, her tail flipping playfully in the air. She swam away from the shore, her scales and mane shimmering in the sunlight as she disappeared into the horizon. Felix looked to Elenora who in turn sighed.

The two began walking down the beach briskly, to catch up with Garmon and relay the bad news. Within a few moments, they found him sitting on the beach, staring off into the distance, and looking extremely worried. He only looked up when Felix and Eleonora were close enough to cast their shadows over his body.

"So, did you figure it out?" Felix asked him.

"What, that we're on an island? Unfortunately, yes," Garmon replied.

"Well, what are we to do now?" Eleonora said softly.

"I guess we need to figure out how to get off this island and onto the mainland. I wish Eleonora and I could just fly, but there is too much wind and I fear that a fish will leap from the water and take us for an insect," Garmon said, standing up and brushing the sand off his body and wings.

"Should we try to build a raft and paddles, then?" Felix asked.

"Might as well. Gather some twigs and leaves. I'll begin tearing up my tunic so we can bind the twigs together."

Garmon began to walk away from the shore and into a patch of trees behind him. Felix and Eleonora followed, picking up various sticks and leaves they found on the sand. Eventually, there was dirt underneath their little feet, and many more twigs were gathered. The three reconvened and Garmon began fashioning a raft by lining up the twigs and binding them together. He had nearly finished when his concentration was interrupted by the shrill voice of Sirenia once again.

"Ha ha! You'll never make it that way! The ocean will eat you right up, and then you will all become fish food!" The messy mass of reddish-brown hair poked up from the surface once more.

"And you will allow us to be swept up by the sea? I thought we had just become friends!" Felix hastily interjected before Garmon could say something rude or disrespectful. Felix felt that they needed the undine's assistance, and her curious interest in them could certainly be used to their advantage.

"You and I are friends, of course. And your lovely faery friend as well. But the grumpy faery owes me an apology—that is, if you want my help getting to the mainland," Sirenia giggled.

"Come on, Garmon. We need her help!" Felix said. Garmon avoided eye contact with him and continued working on the raft, ignoring everyone around him.

"Please, Garmon? Please?" Eleonora stood right in front of him, knelt down, and begged the faery with her hands clasped together. Garmon looked up at her for a moment, then began to crack a smile in the corners of his mouth and finally, let loose an entire grin at Eleonora's hopeful face.

"Well, all right. I'm sorry, Miss Undine..."

"Sirenia."

"I'm sorry, Sirenia..."

"For being rude...?"

"For being rude."

"And I promise never to cross an undine again, as they are surely the cleverest and most beautiful of beings, and are overall better than all other species in general!"

"And... Hey! I'm not saying that!" Garmon looked angrily at the undine, who was laughing uncontrollably.

"It's quite all right," she said. "I got what I wanted from you. And of course you wouldn't repeat that—you're a faery, after all. Seems accurate to what I've heard."

"What exactly have you heard?" Garmon demanded.

"Enough to know why you wouldn't recite those words."

Before Garmon could retort, the undine went under the surface of the water for a moment then resurfaced as close to shore as she could slide without completely beaching herself. She motioned them over to her. As the beings approached, she put out her hand.

"What are we to do with that?" Garmon asked, nodding toward her hand.

"Why, get on it, of course! I'll swim you to shore."

"And you are to hold your hand above the surface for the entire time?" Felix chimed in.

"Uh, no. You can ride atop my head, and grasp onto my hair. I can swim with my head above the surface. It really isn't that far from here. I imagine it would take us only a moment to get to shore, it's about as far as the length of a couple of humpbacks."

"What are humpbacks?" Eleonora asked.

"Whales, of course! You little beings are so funny."

Felix and Eleonora exchanged confused looks, but neither inquired further. Garmon didn't appear to be listening at all, or if he was he hid it quite successfully.

"Before we completely trust you, may I ask what your intentions were in speaking to us initially?" Felix said. "I do not mean any disrespect, but I've heard many tales of undines luring humans to the shore with their hypnotizing song, then drowning to the tune of your euphoric melody." He wore a look of hope upon his face to the undine, so perhaps she would see that he did not mean to be rude, just cautious. After all, he had only met this being just moments before!

"You are not a human, are you?" Sirenia replied.

"Clearly not."

"Then you have nothing to worry about. Undines and humans haven't gotten along for ages. They destroy our ocean, and kill our sea creature friends—so we drown them. Eye for an eye; as we see it, that is. I assure you I have no ill intentions toward you little beings. In fact, I've always found nymphs and faeries to be adorable, and now I am very sure that you are all quite charming!"

"Even Garmon?"

"Even Garmon. Especially Garmon. I've always had a thing for the grumpy ones," Sirenia cooed, winking at the male faery. Garmon looked surprised for a moment, then slowly mustered a smile at the undine.

"Very well, then, we will ride upon your head to shore! You have our trust, Sirenia," Garmon declared, standing up straight and puffing out his chest.

Felix grabbed Eleonora's hand just as he noticed Garmon was reaching to do the very same thing. Eleonora turned pink and clasped her hand into Felix's. Garmon turned his head away from the two and climbed into Sirenia's hand, with Felix and Eleonora right behind him. Sirenia placed the three beings atop her head, and they clutched tightly to clusters of her hair. She took off swimming rapidly through the waves, keeping her head above the water from the nose up.

The three small beings began to see towers of rock cliffs ahead of them after a few precarious moments of dodging the swells atop the undine's head. As they got closer, they could see outlines of trees scattered behind the cliffs. Sirenia sailed into an area with calmer water, sliding her body partially onto the shore. She extended her arm and the beings took turns scaling down her shoulder before leaping onto the sandy shore.

"Thank you, Sirenia!" the three chorused in unison.

"You are very welcome," she replied. "If I am not in this realm to help others, then what am I existing for? Do me a favor though, would you?"

"Anything, Sirenia," Eleonora said.

"Pass the love on. Everybody needs some."

"We will!" Felix called out as Sirenia started to slide away.

The group waved to the undine, who simply smiled at them and backed up into deeper water, bobbing her head above the surface as she waved a final goodbye.

CHAPTER 8

owan sat in the throne room with a black, decrepit book upon his lap, as Caul sprinkled black powder on the ground in a rectangular shape to the king's left. Once the goblin had completed his task, he set four piles of herbs placed at each corner of the rectangle aflame, and wafted the black, billowing smoke toward the center. Then he stood off to Rowan's side with his head bowed. Tiatana sat on Rowan's other side, hands bound and blindfolded. A smirk upon his rotting face, Rowan began to read:

"I call upon thee, Undermost Spirit Gorgon, by the power vested in everlasting chaos—that this portal shall be opened! Seethe and writhe, your underworld creatures! Bring forth your diabolical deeds to seep into the earth of the Forest. Pollute the air with your smoke of deception, Doppel! Destroy the thin veil between the living and the dead, and let your monsters roam freely! Let turmoil and treachery reign supreme through this land! *SO SHALL IT BE!*"

The room shook angrily, as if ancient, underground forces were suddenly shaken out of torpor and forced to emerge from the depths of the earth. The black powder suddenly burst into flame, and the rectangle on the ground emanated a dark red light that seemed to vibrate in a manner all its own. Then the fire erupted, and withdrew forcefully into the ground, leaving a hissing scorched mark that turned to ash and seeped into the ground. The dark red light still flickered, though now it was fading in and out as if it were coming from somewhere very deep below.

"It worked, my liege!" Caul hissed, but his master held up his hand to silence him.

"Time for the sacrifice," Rowan cackled, motioning to his mother. "Surely this will prove my allegiance to the Under Spirits and the delightful heathens we are about to meet."

Caul grabbed Tiatana, and dragged her over to the glowing rectangle as she sobbed and begged for her life. Caul laughed and tossed her straight into the hole. Rowan jerked his head to the side to avoid her fading wails as she fell into the depths of the underworld. Her body slammed to the bottom with a thud, followed immediately by the sound of scuttles and shuffling headed toward her, attracted to the smell of fear and vulnerability.

Rowan stood up, and Caul moved to his side as they anxiously awaited someone—or something—to emerge from the burned rectangular hole in the ground. After what seemed like an eternity to Rowan, reddish-gray smoke began to drift up out of the hole and fill the throne room, mingling with the blackened smoke of the herbs.

"This is it, Caul. The underworld has opened. I've created the doorway, the entrance through which the ghouls and beasts of the underworld shall enter into our realm. Oh, what fun they will have, ridding us of all the meddling beings and finishing off the Forest with darkness, just as Agrimon intended when he possessed Labete. But I did it so much better! How pleased Gorgon will be with me. Perhaps he might even promote me as an Under Spirit to replace Agrimon!

"Once the creatures of the underworld destroy the kingdoms and the Higher Spirits, then there shall be just one absolute ruler of the Forest!" Rowan laughed maniacally.

"And who is that, sire?" Caul asked, his eyes wide.

"Me, you idiot. Me."

"Ah, yes! It shall be you!"

The two continued laughing as monstrous creatures from the hole in the ground began to emerge from their underworld tombs, crawling and writhing out of the doorway, then sliding out of the palace and into the Forest.

One creature looked like a pale, emaciated human, with a triangular face and elongated fingers with jagged joints. It crawled on its stomach across the floor, wriggling away as it gruesomely craned its neck around in all directions.

Another creature emerged that was extremely large and plump, with thick, matted black hair that covered its entire body. It stunk, and left a trail of pus on the ground from its dragging tail as it stomped out of the room—but before leaving, it turned to Rowan and Caul, baring razor sharp teeth that dripped with drool and traces of blood.

Finally, a humanoid figure rose up, standing upright and stepping gently onto the solid ground in front of Rowan and Caul. Though human-like in appearance, the creature was formed by lava, which radiated deep red-and-orange magma underneath the blackest of ash that crusted off as it moved.

"Are you the one who invited us into your realm?" the magma creature boomed at Rowan, and though the creature bore no visible features, Rowan could feel its glare upon him.

"Yes, 'twas I!" Rowan spoke confidently. "I am Rowan, King of the Nymphs!"

"Then I owe you my servitude. Gorgon approves of your quest, Rowan. He is very pleased with the changes you are implementing in the Forest.

"I am Vulcan, and I command all the horrendous entities that emerged before me. Because you freed me from the torturous existence of the underworld, I am forever indebted to you. Your wish is my command, master," the creature thundered.

"Then I command thee to send your minions into the Forest to begin the destruction. Gather any beings that may be suitable sacrifices for the fallen spirits of the underworld. And if anyone resists, they are at the mercy of your creatures," Rowan said. "As for you, Vulcan, I have a special assignment for you."

"What is it, master? My insides thirst for blood of the beings of light!"

"Some prisoners of mine used a portal to escape the palace and are likely headed back toward the palace to save their pathetic friends. Two faeries, a male and female, and a male nymph. Find them, and bring them to me. I have a few lessons to teach them about leaving a party before the games have even begun. It's time they learned some manners."

Rowan scowled his sunken eyes at Vulcan, who bowed his head and nodded at the former nymph. Then Vulcan, lava dripping down his legs, stomped out of the palace, through Nymph Kingdom, and into the Forest, leaving a trail of burning liquid magma in his wake.

"So, why do you think King Alston would have an Elemeportal, anyway?" Eleonora asked as the three walked east, away from the coast.

"Good question," Felix replied. "I would imagine that he does have some practical purpose for it. I just do not happen to know what it is."

"Of course you would say that," Garmon retorted, seemingly grumpy that the topic was even brought up in the first place. "You nymphs are always so quick to defend your weak king. Alston was probably involved with dirty dealings, like the kind you find in the darkest part of the Forest. That's probably why he has so many rare jewels and metals."

"And what would you know about that?" Felix said angrily. "After the falling, Alston traded many of his jewels and improved aspects of Nymph Kingdom. You should really do your research before you open up your big, fat mouth about matters you know nothing about!"

"I've done plenty research. It's a well-known fact in Faery Kingdom that Alston was a terrible king. And everything I've learned recently about him proves it. As far as I know, the Faery King has no dungeon, nor the need to jump elemental dimensions!" Garmon shot back.

"I bet all the kingdoms have one hidden somewhere," Eleonora chimed in, giving Felix sympathetic eyes. "It would make sense, especially if the portal is really that ancient."

Garmon harrumphed. "Stay out of this, Eleonora. Felix just wants to defend Alston because his mommy and daddy were raised by him."

"You mean my 'mommy and daddy' who saved the entire Forest just a generation ago?" Felix replied smugly. "I'm done with this conversation, Garmon, but all I am going to say about it is that it's no surprise you think you know so much about King Alston. You two are a lot alike."

Felix smirked at Garmon and turned his body away from him as he walked. Eleonora looked terrified of the confrontation and stayed beside Felix silently, looking as though she wished that she hadn't prompted the conversation in the first place.

When the three small beings finally reached a stream at the foot of Lapis Mountain, Garmon walked beside the bank while Eleonora and Felix stayed to his side, closer to the trees. They tiptoed over any rough terrain or leaves so as not to make even the slightest of sound.

Following the stream was a wise idea, as it would surely show them the quickest way to pass through the mountain; but the potential danger of what could possibly dwell in or around the stream would cause much more logical beings to avoid the bodies of water altogether. But time was of the essence for the little beings, and thus, they followed the stream.

A large boulder sat halfway submerged in the water, bulging out of the earth and slightly leaning on a flatter rock propped up on its side. Garmon motioned for the two to stay close to him as they passed, because clearly the boulder was blocking their view of what lay on the other side.

The part of the Forest the beings were currently passing through was not of any kingdom of being. It was uninhabited land that foreign witches often transplanted their tree homes into. Subsequently, it was also an area of the Forest which any menacing being that occupied the Forest—yet was not of a species meriting a kingdom of their own—could call their home. Goblins were known to reside in areas like these, though currently it was likely that any goblin that once occupied this area would now be stationed in Nymph Kingdom under Rowan's tyrannical rule.

The three warriors crept quietly past the boulder, and were just about to breathe a sigh of relief when a muddy gray, tall, bipedal creature stepped in front of them, emerging out of a thick blackberry bush that was twisted in a clump around the stream's shore. The creature had an oddly-shaped head, with points protruding from his cheeks, a big, bullfrog-like mouth, and small, black beady eyes. The top of the head was hollow, and a pool of water sloshed back and forth within the hole each time the creature moved. Garmon jumped back and ran right into Felix and Eleonora, who were behind him.

"It's a kalpie," he whispered, conveying a hint of fear in his voice that was very unlike him.

"We have to get it to dump the water out of the hollow in his head," Felix said quickly. "That's the best way to get him to leave us alone. He'll have to return to the stream to replenish his head, and we can run away."

"What if we can't make the water come out?" Eleonora asked, her voice shaky.

"Well, there is one other option," Felix replied.

"What's that?" Garmon grumbled.

"We have to outright kill it."

"Why, hello there, little beings!" the kalpie said. "Don't you look nice and delicious on this fine day!" It took a step forward, sloshing the water in its cranial cavity.

"I hope you've just eaten, Kalpie, because your appetite will need to wait a bit longer for its next meal!" Felix shouted at the creature. The kalpie laughed maniacally. "Don't worry, I'll still have an appetite once I've swallowed your tiny souls. You are but a mere appetizer!"

The kalpie lunged at the beings, who scattered off in different directions, the faeries fluttering off frantically while Felix dove into the blackberry bush. He crawled on his stomach to a thick part impenetrable even to the creature, just before the kalpie thrust its hand into the thorns, narrowly grabbing his little nymph leg.

The kalpie pulled its arm out and spotted Eleonora flying into a patch of leaves on a branch of an oak tree nearby. It charged over in her direction. Felix watched in horror as the kalpie knocked the leaves off the tree, revealing the shivering little faery sitting on the branch, holding a sharp thorn in front of her and waving it around nervously. Felix knew he had to move fast if he was to save Eleonora. He snapped off the longest and thickest thorn he could find and tore a strip of fabric off his tunic. He crawled out of the bush, picked up a hefty twig, and bound it to the thorn with his tunic strip.

The kalpie snatched up Eleonora and squeezed her little body in its hand. It looked over her for a moment, licking its lips and allowing drops of drool to cascade from the corners of its mouth onto the dirt below. Eleonora slammed her eyes shut and whimpered helplessly as the kalpie opened its enormous mouth and held the faery over the gaping entrance to its throat.

Eleonora screamed just as Felix dashed over to the kalpie's feet, zealously stabbing his freshly made spear into the center of the creature's wide, flat right foot. The kalpie wailed and released its grip on Eleonora, who fluttered in the air for a moment, confused, before seeing her opportunity to flee and taking it.

The kalpie looked down at Felix, pouring a few drops of water from its head onto the nymph's, who sliced the spear up out of the foot in one quick motion. The kalpie's blood glimmered on the point of the spear in the waning light of the day just before Felix slammed the spear down once more into the bleeding wound, this time twisting the spear around and ripping apart more flesh.

The kalpie screamed and jumped around, prompting the water in the hollow of its head to splash out in all directions, emptying the hole entirely. Then the kalpie began to shudder uncontrollably. It thrashed around, and jumped head first into the stream as Felix ran as fast as he had ever known to catch up to Eleonora.

CHAPTER 9

"Where were you?" Felix asked Garmon, out of breath from running when he had finally caught up with the two faeries.

"I did what I was taught. I found a suitable hiding spot and assessed the situation. I made a spear similar to the one you're carrying, but you just happened to reach the kalpie first," Garmon snapped, avoiding eye contact with Felix and admiring his own newly-made spear instead.

"So, did you not see that Eleonora was on the verge of being eaten by the kalpie?" Felix asked angrily.

"I told you, I saw everything. If you hadn't been there I would have run out seconds after you and attacked."

"If I hadn't been there Eleonora would be eaten!" Felix nearly yelled. "Did you not know that a kalpie killed my grandmother? They're extremely dangerous!"

Garmon stormed up to Felix, his nose nearly slamming into the nymph's. "Last time I checked, you were a warrior, too. As is she," he said, motioning to Eleonora. "We are trained rigorously to handle situations like this. If you want me to treat you like a baby, I'm happy to, but it won't help us!"

"Please, Garmon," Eleonora broke in, sounding exasperated. "Can't we just agree that it's fortunate we survived that ordeal? We need to keep moving, anyway."

Felix and Garmon looked at one another for a moment, then Garmon backed away, fiddling with the chain around his neck once again and looking extremely frustrated while doing so.

"Follow me," he called back after a moment. "We need to find somewhere to rest for the night before we reach the darkest part of the Forest. I don't know about you two, but I have no desire to travel through that area at night."

Garmon took off, fluttering just above the ground. Felix and Eleonora followed on foot, and Eleonora slyly slipped her hand into Felix's as they walked. Felix turned his face so as not to show the bright red hue it had flushed, and the two traveled behind Garmon, looking around for a good spot to turn in for the night.

"I've found a spot," Garmon said after awhile. He pointed to a hollow under the roots of an old oak tree, and the three shimmied in and made themselves comfortable. Felix and Eleonora cuddled up to each other right away, and Garmon looked visibly uncomfortable at the sight of their obvious contentment. But he quickly settled down and closed his eyes, drifting off to sleep.

Eleonora also fell asleep almost instantly, but Felix found that his mind was having a difficult time calming down enough to allow him to fully rest. His headache started up again, throbbing across his entire brain, and soon he found himself unable to open his eyes all the way. Finally, unable to handle the pain, he stood up and sat near one of the large roots that surrounded them.

Felix... said the voice in his head again, spoken through the headache. Felix, the veil has been lifted. The Forest is haunted. We cannot stay. We must go, before the haunters destroy our light.

Felix squinted his eyes, looking out to the Forest around the shelter. He began to notice some movement in the air coming towards him. It appeared that a towering army of partially see-through spirits was crusading through the thick tree line, not yielding to any form of solid matter as the army drifted through without even the slightest sound.

The spirits were tall—much taller than a nymph, and quite taller than a living human. They had round heads, dark, beady eyes, stocky bodies, and long, thin limbs. As they grew closer, Felix noticed that even though they were partially invisible, and would fade in and out of sharper visibility, that the beings appeared to be made of wood, lined with the kinds of markings that would be apparent on an extremely old and wise oak tree.

"Tree spirits..." Felix whispered to himself. He was shocked at seeing these spirits here, they were well-known throughout the Forest kingdoms as not only being very ancient, but extremely elusive as well.

Tree spirits were inherently good, but generally did not show themselves to beings of the Forest. They remained invisible to the eye yet provided a watchful presence over the Forest, paying specific attention to the trees. These were the spirits that whispered to Nyxen, his mother Ginia, and now, Felix. But they were leaving, and Felix wondered why.

"Please," he implored, taking care not to speak too loudly as to awaken his comrades. "The Forest needs you. Please, don't go,"

A day may come where it will be safe for us to return. But for now, we must go. We are sorry, Felix, grandson of Ginia. There is no other choice.

The tree spirits stomped past the shelter, and yet floated at the same time, in a manner Felix would not have been able to describe adequately even after witnessing the phenomenon with his own eyes.

"This can't be good," he whispered to himself as he watched the tree spirits fade off into the distance. "I guess now we're really on our own."

Felix stared after them long after the darkness of night swept entirely over the Forest. He wanted to sleep, but still simply couldn't. The best thing he could do was make himself useful by continuing to keep watch.

After the Forest was completely dark and no sounds penetrated his ears, Felix again began to notice something strange happening in the trees around the group's hiding spot. Several orbs of grayish-white light darted around among the trees in front of his very eyes.

As he continued watching, the orbs began to form discernible shapes, human figures dashing through the trees, several large ones appearing to be chasing after a smaller one, who looked female in form.

Despite her desperate attempts at escaping the the three large forms, the one being chased fell, just in front of where Felix was standing, landing flat on her face. She lifted her head to look the nymph straight in the eye. Felix held his breath as he looked into the fearful and panicking eyes of the helpless woman, and began to reach his little hand out to her.

Suddenly, just as Felix was about to touch her hand, the woman was violently pulled away from him and dragged across the Forest floor by several ghostly men wearing old-looking petticoats and hats. The woman's mouth was open in a silent scream as the men, their forms emitting a greenish glow, yanked her to her feet. They held her while one of them swung a rope around her neck and tightened it.

The woman's mute screams could almost be heard in Felix's tiny ears as one of the men tossed the other end of the rope around the branch of a tree, and all the men grabbed onto it and pulled as hard as they could, hoisting the woman into the air by her neck. The woman struggled and thrashed about, but finally fell limp, and swung back and forth in the wind, dancing for the men to a soundless melody whispering within the trees.

As quickly as the image faded into view for Felix, it suddenly drifted away, and the nymph found himself staring once again into the darkness of the Forest. His ears rang a shrill tone and his heart pounded out of his chest. He tried not to shudder as he backed away from the edge of the hollow, and lay down beside Eleonora once more. He closed his eyes, hoping to fall asleep this time but knowing full well that he probably wouldn't.

CHAPTER 10

In the Nymph Palace dungeon, Myso and Basil had been confined in a cell together with Narena and Kellen for quite some time. The damp, dark dungeon was beginning to take its toll on the hopeful natures of the beings, and lack of food and water was making them very weak. Narena laid her head on Kellen's stomach, and he on the skunk's tail, who was curled in a ball beside Myso, sitting cross-legged in the corner meditating.

Out of nowhere, Basil leapt up, tossing Kellen and Narena up a few inches before they landed on their bottoms upon the cold, hard ground.

"Hey!" Narena cried, rubbing her rear end as she stood up in surprise.

"Sorry, sorry. I had the strangest dream. I was shaken out of it all of a sudden, like I was supposed to wake up at that exact moment," Basil said with a hint of confusion in his voice.

"What was the dream about?" Myso said from the corner, looking intrigued.

"I was speaking to a deer. Except the deer was white, sprinkled with gold bits. And... its mouth didn't move when it spoke. I just heard what it was saying within my mind."

"Well, then? What did it say to you, Basil?" Myso's lavender eyes were nearly popping out of his head with interest.

"It said that our missing friends are alive, and journeying back to us, with the intention of rescuing us and all of Nymph Kingdom," Basil replied as he looked around awkwardly.

"And?" Myso leaned over in anticipation.

"And, well, um, Rowan and the goblins unleashed quite a few dark entities on the Forest. And... they may have broken the barriers between our realm and the underworld."

"They may have? Or they have?"

"They have. Definitely have."

"That doesn't sound good," Narena said, turning to look into Kellen's green eyes.

"But why a deer?" Basil asked.

"It's not an actual deer, silly!" Myso exclaimed.

"It's a Higher Spirit! You spoke to a Higher Spirit!" Narena interrupted, her eyes wide with excitement. "The Yew was white and glittered in gold as well!"

"Wait, I thought Higher Spirits were forbidden to speak," Kellen interjected.

"Well, like I said, it didn't speak aloud," Basil replied. "I just somehow inherently knew what it was saying. Within my thoughts. I guess that's how I 'heard' it."

"It weakens Higher Spirits to speak," Narena continued. "They are solely supposed to do what it is they are specified in—loving, guiding, protecting, or directing. They do this through unspoken influence, visions, or signs... Never through speaking! You remember this, don't you Kellen? Hawthorne told us about it before he died."

"I guess I must have forgotten," Kellen grumbled. "It's been a long time, and I was hoping something like this wouldn't happen again. And why are you all so excited about this? Normal beings interacting with the Higher Spirits so nonchalantly is what led to Labete's demise. Now our Forest lacks a Higher Spirit to protect, which is likely why it was so easy for Rowan to take over in the first place!"

"If it was a deer, it must have been Sator!" Narena exclaimed, ignoring her husband's rant—something she'd grown quite good at. "Sator directs, so he had to have been directing Basil to do something. Thus far he has only told us what is going on outside of this dungeon! There had to have been something else!"

"How do you know Sator is a deer?" Basil inquired.

"The Spirits of the Forest have to show themselves in the likenesses of other Forest inhabitants," Myso chimed in. "In reality, they really resemble nothing—for they are Spirits—but when they must appear, they do in some form. Do you know the other forms, Narena?"

"I do. I read about it once in the Forest Grimoire. The Yew is a crow, Sator is a deer, Arepo is a turtle." She paused. "Although I've heard that sometimes Arepo shows himself as a fish. Oh, and Labete is a salamander... er, *was* a salamander."

"And now the salamanders are all gone from this Forest," Myso whispered. "And so is Labete." He looked over to Narena, and noticed the tears start to well in her eyes. "Sorry, Narena," he said quietly.

"It's okay," she mumbled back. "Hawthorne was the last salamander before he died. Oh, Yew, how I miss him."

"What about the Under Spirits?" Basil spoke up, eager to change the subject for Narena's sake. "Do they show themselves in the form of Forest dwellers?"

"Yes, but not animals," Narena went on. "And as far as I know, nobody has seen them in their visible forms for hundreds of generations. The Grimoire merely speculates on their appearance based on ancient tales. Gorgon is an ogre, Doppel is a goblin, Valerian is a reebob, and Agrimon is—I mean, was—a kalpie."

"And yet, there are still kalpies about the Forest," Kellen muttered to no one in particular. "Even after the falling."

"But wait, Basil," Myso broke in. "What exactly did Sator direct you to do, then?"

"Um, remember that goblin that is always around Rowan?" Basil said quietly as the other three leaned in closer and huddled around him.

"Yes, I believe his name is Caul," Myso replied. "What about him?"

"Well... Um..."

"Spit it out, Basil!" the troll hissed impatiently.

"One of us has to kill him. Only then will our friends be unimpeded in their attempt to destroy Rowan and close the doorway to the underworld."

"All we need to do is slay one goblin and my son will succeed? Sounds easy enough to me," Kellen said.

"Well, Sator didn't say anything about that being a sure thing. Killing Caul would only make it truly possible for Felix and the others to even get to Rowan," Basil replied.

"So the real problem is then, how are we to slay Caul in our current predicament?" Narena said. "I can try to meditate and use my seer sight that was given to me by Hawthorne to find out, but with my mind so frazzled over everything that's happened recently, I can't guarantee complete accuracy. But I can try."

"We'll just have to wait for the first good opportunity and go from there," Kellen declared. "In the meantime, why don't we try to rest up some more? We're exerting a lot of energy with all this excitement that we could be using to get out of here when the opportunity arises."

"Always thinking like a true warrior," Narena beamed at her husband, cuddling up to him as he lay down and closed his eyes. "But I am far too excited to sleep. Will you talk with me, Myso? That should help me calm down enough to meditate properly."

Myso's large, pointed ears perked up. "Sure, Narena. What is it you would like to know?" The troll's eyes were closed, but a slight smile spread across his face.

"Why did you decide to become a warrior?"

Myso paused for a moment, and gathered his thoughts the best he could. He had not spoken much about his past to many beings in his lifetime, though not because he hadn't wanted to. It was simply that up until this point, no one he had come across had ever really cared to ask. That is, except Basil, who knew everything there was to know about his troll friend but was trustworthy enough to keep the information to himself.

"Well, I guess the reason I became a warrior was to show my father that I was something, you know? Something more than what he thought I was, I suppose."

"Was your father unkind to you while you were growing up?"

"Not really. He was never unkind, just unfeeling in general. He gave me no outward love, though I bite my tongue if his intentions were to. I just simply never felt anything from him. It was often as if I didn't exist at all, really."

"That's so sad. I'm sorry."

"Don't be. It has made me who I am today. And I've found family in my friends," Myso said, cocking his head over in Basil's direction.

Narena's eyes were wide open, so she took notice, and her attention was then drawn to the skunk who was now audibly snoring to her side.

"What about Basil? What's his story?" Narena asked, her voice low.

The troll opened his eyes slightly to check if Basil was awake, but upon finding that his friend certainly wasn't, cleared his throat.

"Basil's had a tough life. He was the runt of his litter, and, like myself, did not experience much love from his parents when he was growing up. Aside from that, his siblings tormented him daily, and he was constantly told that he was weak by his peers. He doesn't care much for his own kind nowadays, if you can imagine! That's why he asked to be stationed in a kingdom that did not have any other skunks in the army, hence—how he found Troll Kingdom. And that's how we became such good friends. I'm lucky to have found him."

"Certainly so!" Narena exclaimed.

Myso closed his eyes once again and Narena followed suit. But her mind was filled with endless thoughts that impeded her ability to meditate properly. She felt good that she now had a better understanding of the beings whom she was imprisoned with—even though she had known that she liked them from the very start—and found through hearing their stories that she now enjoyed their existences even more than she had before.

Narena also felt grateful that she had imparted the kind of love upon her only son that Myso and Basil, as well as herself, had lacked growing up. Narena could relate to them in an odd sense. Her parents had passed away when she was quite young, and she had mainly known the love of her brother and animal friends growing up, even despite being raised in the palace with Alston, Tiatana, and Rowan. Whether the royal family had indeed actually loved her and Nyxen was debatable; and Narena was more inclined to think they took her in more out of pity and a responsibility to her parents than anything else, especially love. Her parents had saved Alston's life, given their lives for his, and Narena couldn't help but resent the king for living when her parents hadn't been provided such a luxury.

But still, despite her parents being gone, she had indeed felt their love, albeit in a strange way. But like-minds seem to attract other like-minds, and Narena couldn't help but wonder if it was once again fated for her to be in the exact right place, at the exact right time, in order to help save her beloved Forest once again. She just hoped Felix had met a similar fate.

CHAPTER 11

The next morning the three small beings awoke with the sunrise, and Felix was pleasantly surprised to find that he had indeed fallen asleep the night before. He decided not to speak of the ghostly vision he witnessed, as he had no desire to frighten Eleonora after her ordeal the day before with the kalpie, and no good could ever come of telling something like that to Garmon.

Felix was tired of their arguing, and intuitively felt that it was his duty to keep peace if Garmon wouldn't. And since the likelihood of Garmon being agreeable with Felix was slim to none, Felix opted to try, from then on, to be the bigger being.

Garmon emerged from their shelter first, and stretched his arms and legs.

"Wow, it's windy," he commented, to which Eleonora and Felix nodded in agreement. "Did you notice how freezing cold it was last night? I could barely keep warm."

"I shivered almost the whole night," Eleonora added. "Luckily I slept close to Felix, he kept me warm."

Garmon harrumphed. "I have a warm body, too, you know," he grumbled.

"Yes, but you slept all the way in the corner," Eleonora replied. "Felix was right there next to me."

"He always is," Garmon groaned. "Let's get moving."

The three continued their journey, and after a short while they found themselves at the entrance to the darkest part of the Forest.

"We need to be extra careful here," Felix whispered to the two faeries. "I've heard from my parents and grandfather that this is not an area of the Forest to underestimate. Even though it's daytime, there's still a chance we could run into negative entities. And they're not always visible to the naked eye, so we need to pay close attention to all our senses."

"Yeah, yeah," Garmon mocked. "We know, Felix."

"I'm serious, Garmon," Felix replied. "This is for our own protection. Your brazenness is something that will not be appreciated here. We can't risk anything—there's already too many unknowns."

"Well, the longer we stand around here talking, the more likely we are to be noticed. Let's just go!" Garmon ordered. Felix let out a sigh but obliged, clutching onto Eleonora's hand.

The oak trees in the thickest part of the Forest were enormous, and very ancient. Their gnarled branches hung low, covering the sky entirely so that no sunshine or hint of blue could venture to the near-blackness at Forest floor where the beings walked. The air was thick and cold; the feeling of invisible eyes watched at all times, and barely-noticeable shadows darted around in every direction.

The three stuck close to each other, collectively jumping each time a snarl, growl, whoop, or whistle was heard. The whistling was the most unnerving, as the pitch seemed to follow them and, at times, sounded as if it were addressing them. When the whistling sounded as though it was coming from a thick bramble bush the group was attempting to pass through, Garmon had finally had enough.

"Whoever is whistling at us, I demand that you show yourself, so that we can fight fairly!" the faery shouted into the abyss of the bush. There was no response, only silence. But when the three began to trudge on once more, the whistle sounded again.

Garmon stopped mid-step and looked around with a mixture of anger and exasperation on his face.

"Please don't say anything more, Garmon. Nothing about this part of the Forest is fair. Thus far we have been treated with respect as we pass through. I do not want to lose that, as we would surely be faced with something more sinister than a simple whistler!" Felix looked softly at the faery, and for the first time, Garmon returned his expression not with indignation, but with a mostly blank stare.

"Fine. I will try to ignore the noises from now on," Garmon sighed.

In this particular Forest, faeries were known for having a difficult time dealing with their emotions. In fact, faeries have the potential to be so feisty that many experience difficulties in harboring more than one strong emotion at any given time, and therefore often lack the ability to reason or problem-solve under pressure. Felix was aware of this—he'd experienced it many times in his childhood when his faery aunt, Sebillon, would give his uncle, Nyxen, a hard time about whatever whim she was chasing that particular day.

Nyxen had always handled it well, using a mix of self-deprecating humor and sympathetic shoulder rubs to turn Sebillon's mood around, and it worked, for the most part. But faeries' ever-changing moods were another reason that Felix felt slighted at Garmon's lead warrior status over him. Nymphs were much better problem solvers than faeries, but the extensive reign of King Alston's ignorance prompted a bad reputation for nymphs throughout the Forest's kingdoms—especially among the faeries, who were still very discriminatory, despite all the changes and revelations that came to the Forest in the aftermath of the falling. Felix hoped to change some of those views to create a better existence within the Forest for the nymphs. But first, he would have to create a better existence for himself.

"Felix, what's that?"

Felix's thoughts were interrupted by Eleonora's shaky voice. He quickly turned to see a small male being, old and bearded. He slowly sauntered past them, seeming to float in thin air. He wore a tall, pointed, red hat and thick brown boots, and in his hand, he carried a large, pointed, deep purple crystal. He paid no mind to the beings, his saunter turning into a skip as he drifted by.

"Excuse me, Gnome?" Garmon asked aloud, but the gnome ignored him, continuing on his way. Garmon stomped after him. "Gnome? *Gnome?* HELLO?"

"He can't hear you," Felix called out. "Can't you tell? And look at him, he's partially see-through!"

"Is he... a ghost?" Eleonora squeaked out.

"That's what I think," Felix replied. "There are ghosts everywhere now."

Eleonora darted into a bramble bush, with Felix close behind her. "What's wrong, Eleonora?" the male nymph asked.

"Nothing. I just, well, I'm kind of afraid of ghosts," Eleonora whimpered. "Funny, isn't it? How I can be a warrior and yet still be scared of ghouls." She chuckled nervously.

"Everything will be fine," Felix assured. "It looks like that gnome was just a manifestation of a past event in the Forest. Not an intelligent spirit, otherwise he would have responded to us or at least acknowledged us. His manifestation is likely just going through its routine, over and over again."

"But why would it do that?"

"Something is allowing it to. Something changed in the Forest, and I think there are a lot more ghosts and manifestations than just this one gnome."

Eleonora shuddered. "I wish we didn't have to travel through the Forest anymore. I wish we were home."

"Me too," Felix replied, and put his arm around the female faery. "I wish I knew how my parents, Myso, and Basil were doing."

"It's just a ghost," Garmon declared, interrupting Felix as he crawled into the bush. "What are you guys doing? Kissing?"

"No, Garmon," Felix replied, annoyed. "Eleonora was frightened."

"Are you okay, Eleonora?" Garmon asked, though his tone didn't convey any form of worry behind it.

"I'm fine now," Eleonora replied.

"All right. Let's go."

The nymph and faeries emerged from the bramble bush, and found, to their surprise, that it was now eerily quiet in the dark part of the Forest. No longer were there whoops, growls, or even whistles. There was not even the hiss of the passing wind. Only pure silence, except for the slight crunching of dirt and twigs beneath the beings' feet.

Garmon kept the lead, while Felix and Eleonora stayed close to each other behind him. The three approached an area that was fairly rocky terrain, and the faeries' patience was tested as Felix had a difficult time scaling over the rocks. Garmon, of course, fluttered easily over them, but Eleonora refused to do the same since Felix could not, so the two climbed over the rugged topography hand in hand, as usual.

"Having a difficult time?" a croaky voice sounded over the rocks into the little beings' ears.

"That depends on who's asking!" Felix replied, struggling for breath.

"I mean you no harm, Nymph, unless you mistake me for one of these rocks and step upon my head!"

Two glazed, chartreuse eyeballs emerged from the soil amongst a pile of pebbles in between two larger rocks that Felix and Eleonora were attempting to scale. The dirt quivered, and a coarse, warty face with a wide mouth emerged from nearly underneath them. Felix stopped and looked down at the terrestrial amphibian.

"Hello there, Toad. Are you simply being polite and saying hello, or is there something ahead we should be forewarned of?" Felix spoke assertively, and despite his love of other species, wasn't currently in the state of mind to make a new friend.

"I know not of what lies ahead. I just happened to glance out of my hiding spot here and noticed how exhausted you appear to be. I'm not typically one to volunteer my help, especially in this part of the Forest, but you so resemble an old friend of mine that my gut feeling was to help you. I am Brutus."

"And what do you intend to help with?" Garmon nearly shouted from where he had stopped to listen just moments before, upon noticing that his comrades had halted behind him.

"Clearly you are able to move around this terrain with ease, Faery. I am speaking to this nymph here," the toad curtly replied, and Felix couldn't help but crack a smile.

"How can you help me, Brutus?" Felix asked the toad.

"I know of a burrowing rat who resides in this area. I'm sure he would be happy to assist you by guiding your way through his underground tunnels to wherever you are going. The tunnels are much easier to travel than the Forest in its newly haunted state. But I'm afraid his services come at a price."

"A rat?!" Garmon guffawed, and slapped his knee in amusement.

"What is the price?" Felix asked, ignoring Garmon.

"That I do not know. I have never actually used his services, you see."

"I'm confused as to what it is you actually *do* know, Toad," Garmon snapped. "We do not need the assistance of a burrowing rat. We are doing just fine on our own, thank you very much."

"Suit yourselves. Just thought I'd try to help. If you change your mind, the rat lives under the black oak tree. You will know it when you see it, trust me."

Brutus yawned and snuggled back into the dirt, glancing at Felix one last time before closing his chartreuse eyes and disappearing once again into the soil.

As the three walked away from Brutus, Felix began to feel an overwhelming feeling of anger towards Garmon.

Why is it, Felix thought to himself as he furrowed his brow, that Garmon would do everything in his power to actively go against anything associated with me? Brutus was only trying to help, something that was breath of fresh air in such a harrowing location as the darkest part of the Forest. I'm getting real sick of his attitude, and I don't know how much more of it I can stand.

Perhaps it was their location that prompted such strong feelings within Felix's mind. The darkest part of the Forest was seething with negativity, and surely there were countless entities lurking about with an agenda of negative influence upon impressionable little beings. Felix began to realize this, and turned the focus of his attention on watching Eleonora as she moved, desperately seeking some positive thoughts to rid his mind of the evil that was attempting to creep within it.

Suddenly, within his mind, Felix heard a hissing voice—and a very persuasive one at that, whisper.

Give in. Hurt him. Destroy him. Felix shook his head, trying to drive the thoughts away.

No. I am not that kind, Felix fervently thought back.

What do you have to lose? And who would even notice? His demise could be the result of any entity that dwells within this part of the Forest.

No.

Then no one would stand in your way for the desire of Eleonora.

Do not bring her into this. If anything, it's because of my love for her that I deny such violence.

You'd impress her.

Be gone from my mind, evil spirit. Your influence has no merit here, and I have no intention of entertaining your ridiculousness.

Oh well. Suit yourself. You're all going to die anyway.

At least I would die with love in my heart, Felix replied within his mind.

To his surprise, he found that he no longer heard the whispering thoughts in his head. Then a small, soft hand slipped into his. Felix felt his body flush, and clutched onto Eleonora's hand as the three continued their journey through the darkest and most negative part of the Forest.

CHAPTER 12

yso, Basil, Narena, and Kellen were lying around their dungeon cell when the sound of dragging footsteps approached. They did not know which cell the being was heading for, but all took in a deep breath in the event that it was theirs. Many nymphs and various beings were being held in cells surrounding the group's, but that their cell was of the most importance to Rowan was something they all intuitively knew.

"It's you, Myso," Narena whispered softly to the troll beside her. "I saw it in my meditation. It's all up to you."

"Just me?" Myso replied. "You didn't see anyone else with me?"

"I'm afraid not," she replied, rubbing Myso's arm comfortingly. "But don't worry. You'll be fine. Sator will be with you. I just wish I could put a protective barrier around you, but the goblin would be able to see it and make you break through it."

"It's okay," Myso replied. "You're lucky you can even do that. That ability might come in handy later."

The dragging footsteps drew closer, and now it was apparent that a goblin was indeed approaching their cell. Whether or not it was Caul, the beings were soon to discover. Narena scooted closer to Kellen and clutched his arm tightly, and he in turn slid on his rear to sit in front of her, keeping his hand at her side. Basil and Myso crouched together, the skunk's teeth bared and the troll's body puffed up.

"Hello, prisoners. I'm afraid I must break up your pity party here, but Rowan desires the audience of the troll for a moment. Come with me, Troll."

Myso and Narena exchanged glances. "Good luck," Narena hissed.

The goblin was indeed Caul, and the four beings all stared at each other, eyes wide in horror, at the thought that Myso would in fact be the one to have the most auspicious opportunity to enact Sator's directions. Myso was known to be a kindhearted individual despite his warrior status, and he too felt his heart sink as he fully ascertained that he would be the one to have to kill Caul—and on his own, no less.

"Why me?" Myso questioned as Caul latched his spindly fingers around his bicep.

"Take it up with the king," Caul snapped back.

"And what if I refuse?"

Caul snickered. "It'll be troll for dinner tonight, then, for us goblins! One of our favorite meals!" He made lapping sounds with his tongue, causing Narena to gasp and whimper.

"I do not intend to obey Rowan in any form," Myso went on, "but for the sake of my friends I will go."

"Good choice," Caul sneered and led Myso out of the cell, locking the door behind them.

"I just never thought the goblins were a species to answer to another, let alone smaller, weaker beings," Myso mumbled to the goblin as they started up the steps. But to Myso's shock, Caul did not reply, and instead swung his lanky leg around to knock the troll violently down onto the bottom step.

"Who's the weak one, now?"

Myso said nothing and picked himself up, his blood boiling with anger and embarrassment. Maybe killing Caul would perhaps not be as difficult morally as the troll had previously thought.

Caul led Myso up the stairs, keeping his jagged spear pointed at his back as they ascended into the hallway, then through the foyer. Myso's eyes darted about, looking for an opportunity to catch Caul off guard, but didn't feel like the time was promising. Once they entered the throne room, Rowan was seated, crown upon his decomposing head, slumped in the throne. He looked at Myso with piercing eyes.

"Very good, Caul. Now I demand some privacy with the troll," Rowan said in a gruff voice.

"Yes, sire."

Caul slunk backwards out of the room, leaving Myso and Rowan staring at each other in silence. Rowan righted himself in the throne, cracked his cervical vertebrae audibly, then glared up and down at the troll.

"I've brought you here to make a deal. You help me find those faeries and nymph that you were with, and I will grant you immunity to the horrors I've unleashed upon the Forest," Rowan declared, squinting his eyes under his furrowed brow.

"Did you mean to say that I am here for you to offer a bribe? Because I would never fathom making a deal with someone so evil." Myso wished he had chosen his words better, but trolls were known to be sassy in their straightforwardness, and often blurted out sentences in a manner not always intended.

"I had always thought trolls to be ones eager for a bargain," Rowan replied calmly. "Refuse my olive branch, and you will no longer see my good nature."

"What you refer to as 'good nature' would only be seen in the underworld. I shall not yield on my faith in my friends."

"Then you are foolish indeed. Your mining ancestors were much smarter than you."

"Why, because they unknowingly unleashed beings like you?" Myso said, referring to a time long ago, when a simple mining troll brought forth dark entities out of a careless, love-fueled action. The miner had stolen a jewel and given it to his love, only to find that she'd already given her heart to another.

"So you deny my offer to you?"

"Oh, more than that, Rowan. I spit upon your offer to me." Myso spat on the ground to prove his point.

"Caul!" Rowan hollered, avoiding eye contact with Myso. "Remove this wretched being from my sight!"

Caul entered the room and herded Myso out. Once they were out of Rowan's sight, Myso knew that this would probably be his only opportunity to take the goblin down. Even if he wasn't able to get him on the walk back to his cell, he could enlist the help of his friends to attack once the cell door was opened.

Caul poked Myso with the blunt end of his spear. He seemed frantic somehow, and anxious for reasons the troll couldn't comprehend. Perhaps it was because the goblin knew that Rowan would be angered by the troll's refusal of his deal. Or perhaps he feared the possibility that the beings unaccounted for could be the key to defeating Rowan's terrifying reign. Perhaps, even—though wholly far-fetched—Caul was aware that his time as a living being in the Forest realm was soon to come to an end. But for whatever reason, Caul seemed on edge, and Myso planned on taking advantage of just that.

Please, Higher Spirits, Myso thought. *Forgive me for what I am about to do.* Myso had always thought such a prayer before entering a potentially volatile situation, and despite the Higher Spirits' disdain for goblins, still wanted to do so just in case.

When the two reached the entrance to the dungeon staircase, Caul paused for a moment before motioning for the troll to walk ahead of him. Myso began to descend the stone steps, watching the goblin out of the corner of his eye for any weaknesses. When they were halfway down, Myso noticed that Caul stumbled a bit, so he whipped his body around, swung his leg under the goblin's, and knocked him off his feet. Caul slammed into the stairs, wailing in pain and dropping his spear, which tumbled down the staircase and tapped to a halt at the bottom.

Myso stood above the fallen goblin, looked him straight into his lifeless, gray eyes. Then he grabbed Caul's writhing body and threw it down the on the stairs. It made a moist, crunching sound as it slumped heavily against the corner of the step. Myso then perfected his footing, aimed one of his large, calloused, troll feet directly into Caul's abdomen, and kicked the goblin down the stairs as hard as he could.

The goblin's body crashed into each step, crunching with each impact, until it finally lay on the dungeon floor amid a pool of dark, sticky blood that trailed from the fallen body all the way back up the stairs to Myso's feet.

Myso ran down the staircase, carefully avoiding the trail of blood, and kicked the spear away from Caul's unmoving body. He dashed after it, picked it up, and held it over the fallen monster. Caul wasn't breathing, yet

Myso knew that he could still very well be alive. He would have to ensure that the goblin's head never again lifted from its resting point. Myso kicked Caul so he was lying on his back, and in one swift movement, forcefully stabbed the spear into his heart. His cries of anguish over having killed a being echoed through the cells and crevices of the dungeon. The goblin's body jolted slightly, but then became eerily still and silent.

Myso waited for a moment, staring at his fallen foe, now ambivalent about having to kill but still glad the ordeal was now over. Myso then saw the keys that dangled from the pocket of Caul's now-ripped and bloodied cutoff pants. He quickly reached down, grabbed the keys, and began frantically opening cells—starting with the one that imprisoned his friends.

CHAPTER 13

elix, Garmon, and Eleonora had traveled through most of the darkest region of the Forest. They stopped to rest for a few moments before venturing through the final few lines of trees. Soon they would reach an area less threatening, but the Forest was still potentially dangerous nonetheless. Exhausted and ready for a rest, Felix sat down close beside Eleonora on a large, smooth pebble.

"I wonder where that black oak is," he said dreamily.

"Traveling underground is actually a good idea, in my opinion," Eleonora replied. "If there are ghosts, goblins, and Yew knows what else out here, I'd rather avoid them altogether."

Eleonora spoke loudly enough so that Garmon, who was sitting on a piece of bark just mere steps away from them, could hear. The faery's ears perked up, and he rose from his seat and walked over to where the two were sitting.

"I've decided we will travel underground, for the sake of our safety. We've experienced much in this treacherous journey, and my main objective now is to get us back to Nymph Kingdom without so much as a hiccup along the way. We will find the black oak!" Garmon declared, looking proud of himself.

Eleonora beamed back at him, and though Felix was tempted to roll his eyes decided against it, and instead simply nodded in agreement.

"But how are we to find the black oak?" Eleonora questioned.

"And what if we already passed it?" Felix said.

"The toad, if I remember correctly, said that we would know it when we saw it. I don't know about you two, but I have yet to see any oak tree that looked overly black. But then again, everything in this part of the Forest is dark," Garmon replied.

"What if we just kept going forward in the direction we were going? If we see the oak, great. Then we can solicit the aid of the rat. But if not, we just travel our original way, above-ground. What do you think, Garmon?"

Felix looked at the faery hopefully, wanting in his little nymph heart to believe that Garmon didn't just think all his ideas were bad based on the principle that it was he who was sharing them. He wanted, in some way, to make the idea seem as though it were Garmon's, thus increasing the chances of the faery responding in an agreeable manner.

"Well, that sounds as good idea as any. So it shall be, then. We will trudge onward." Garmon took the lead once again, fiddling with the chain around his neck. The three walked on.

Felix stared at Garmon in confusion. He was surprised by the male faery's immediate acquiescence to his suggestion, and was certainly not expecting it. Garmon was unpredictable, something that Felix was not quite used to, as he had grown up with parents who he could always count on to respond or act a certain way. He feared that Garmon's unpredictability might be seen as endearing to Eleonora, as females often fancied males who harbored aspects of mystery to them; but he assured himself that in Garmon's case, it was not, in fact, endearing, but oddly unsettling, and bordered more on multiple personalities.

When light began to seep between the branches of the trees, the three knew they were approaching the end point to the dark part of the Forest. Felix felt slightly disappointed that they had yet to see the black oak, but was a firm believer that everything happened for a reason, so assumed he was not meant to take the easy way out his journey. They had but one corner to turn before the last line of trees, and right as they turned that corner they were greeted with a magnificent sight.

An ancient oak tree, barren of leaves, stood triumphantly in front of them, its branches mangled and twisting from the canopy to the Forest floor. Its roots burst forth from the earth, resembling a prematurely-buried human crawling up from the depths of the dirt, pulling outward from the tree as if attempting to escape the underworld. The tree itself was a deep shade of black, scorched upon the length of the trunk as though it had just barely survived a Forest fire long ago.

"This must be it," Felix whispered, to which Eleonora nodded and squeezed his hand.

"I would have to agree with you on that one, Felix," Garmon declared. "Now how do we locate the burrowing rat?"

"I know. Why don't you just make a loud ruckus outside his home? You three got it right."

A squeaky yet gruff voice sounded out from under one of the tree's roots. A very plump brown rat emerged and approached the little beings. He sniffed each one up and down for a moment, then bored his small, black, beady eyes into Felix. Felix shifted around uncomfortably, but kept a smile upon his face.

"I'm sorry, sir," Eleonora said kindly. "Did we wake you?"

"We weren't really being that loud," Garmon mumbled.

"Obviously you are hard of hearing, then," the rat snapped. "I could hear you all the way down in my tunnel. I hope you don't call yourselves warriors of any kind. I'd hate to have you fighting on my side."

"And what if we *are* warriors?" Garmon argued. "I'll have you know that I am one of the best faery spear warriors in the entire Forest, if not the best."

"Could have fooled me," the rat replied.

"What's your name, sir?" Eleonora interjected.

"I do not share it with customers. Only with my friends. Just business you see. You understand, I'm sure," the rat replied, stopping between each sentence to sniff the air around him.

"Then what do we call you?" Eleonora questioned.

"Mr. Rat will do quite nicely. Works for every other customer."

"Very well," Felix replied.

"Now, before we leave, there's just one last thing we need to take care of."

The rat slumped backwards, and balanced on the base of his tail as he rubbed his little rodent hands together.

"Which is?" Garmon said, halfway hoping he could intimidate the rodent out of his usual price to be paid, whatever it may be.

"My payment, of course! What, you think I make a living doing this kind of thing for free? Especially now, what with all the goblins and ghouls and all!"

"Ah, yes. What might that payment be?" Felix asked.

"Depends on the customer. What is it that you are able to offer me?"

"Well, we do not have anything on us except for our recently made spears. But if you would like us to fashion you a weapon of sorts, we would be happy to do so—so long as you hold up your end of the bargain," Felix replied.

"Perhaps, but my incisors act as spears within my mouth already. I have no need to carry any unnecessary items with me through the tunnels," the rat said, rubbing his neck with one hand.

"Then how are we to pay you?" Garmon retorted.

The rat studied each of the beings very carefully, sniffing the air in front of them and pacing around them in a circle. His heavy tail dragged across the Forest floor, leaving a trail behind him.

"I have an idea. Wings. Faery wings. I can sell them to witches for things that I may actually need. That's it! If one of you faeries surrenders your wings to me by the end of our underground journey, I will consider the debt repaid. But if you do not, I'm afraid you will pay for the travel with one of your lives." The rat looked from Garmon to Eleonora, and back again.

"What on earth would witches want with faery wings?!" Felix asked angrily. He had seen the look of despair flush over Eleonora's face.

"How should I know? Magic potions, maybe? What they do with them doesn't matter to me. Now, do you accept the deal or not?" the rat snuffed, glaring at the small beings.

"I cannot accept such an offer. It's offensive that you would even consider that a possibility!" Felix said fervently, trying to control his emotions but finding it very difficult.

"You may not have a choice. Look behind you!"

The small beings whirled around to see an enormous black beast, covered in thick fur and heaving hot, stinking breath in their direction as it bared its long, pointed fangs. Eleonora smashed her hand over her nose and whimpered at the horrible stench the creature emanated. "Oh no!" she cried.

"Follow if you want, but the deal still stands!" the rat wailed, and darted back into the root of the black oak tree.

"He's blocking our way back! We don't have a choice, we must go through the tunnels!" Garmon shouted.

Felix hesitated for a moment. Face the huge beast, which likely was a dark entity from the underworld, or travel safely underground, and either Eleonora or Garmon would have to surrender their wings. It was a horrible predicament.

Eleonora and Garmon showed no such hesitation, however. Garmon had already fled into the hole, and Eleonora was dashing after him. Felix had no desire to be separated from the two faeries and face the monster alone. And if the two were agreeing to the deal... well, it was their wings that were in question. Felix decided not to think about it anymore. He ran after his friends as fast as he possibly could without looking back, and dove legs first into the black abyss of the hole.

CHAPTER 14

yso had opened all the doors of the cells in the Nymph Palace dungeon, and the little beings who had previously been confined scooted off in different directions. Some opted to return to their homes and barricade themselves within, while others swore they were fleeing from the kingdom indefinitely. Only Myso, Basil, Narena, and Kellen remained in the dungeon.

"What should we do?" Basil asked. "Do we stay here and try to stop Rowan, or should we try to find Felix, Eleonora, and Garmon?"

"Sator directed us to kill Caul, and remember that killing Caul would make it possible for Felix, Eleonora, and Garmon to defeat Rowan," Myso said. "That says to me that we are not destined to go up against Rowan. The others are."

"All we can do is make it easier for them to succeed," Narena added. "And do whatever we can to further help them."

"I don't know about you guys, but I'm ready to get out of his Gorgon-forsaken hole and do whatever I can to help my son," Kellen chimed in. "This was the first step," he added, motioning to Caul's lifeless body. "Now the fun *really* starts."

"But where are we to go?" Basil asked.

"Let's go to my house," Kellen replied. "Then we can stock up on weapons and replenish our bodies with some food and water."

"I think we should seek some magical help after that," Narena spoke up. "It's worked for us in the past, and my deepest intuitive feelings say that it could really benefit us."

"Sounds good to me," Myso said. "Let's get out of here."

The four quietly crept up the staircase, through the hallway, foyer, and out of the palace unnoticed. When they finally could feel the fresh air upon their faces, they quickly ran for cover, as a group, back to Kellen and Narena's tree home. Kellen scooted everyone inside, keeping watch, and entered last, motioning for all to go into the bedroom, as the front door was still broken down in the entrance to the home. Everyone obliged, and Kellen quietly shut the door and locked it behind them.

"Grab a weapon for yourselves," he whispered. "Some are under the bed, others in the closet. I had some others by the door, but I imagine they were destroyed when the tree came through. It isn't worth the risk to go out there and try to find them in that rubble, anyway. I have plenty more weapons in here."

"That's my guy!" Narena declared with a huge grin, putting her arm around Kellen's waist and resting her head upon his shoulder. "Always a true warrior, staying prepared for anything."

Myso pulled out a long spear from under the bed, smiling as he admired its workmanship, and secured it to his waistband. Kellen made sure he had ample arrows to pair with his bow, and Narena tied a long blade, sheathed within a thick belt, to her waist. Then everyone—except

Basil of course—slid a smaller sheathed blade into one of their boots.

"Let's rest up here for a bit," Kellen announced. "I'll go grab some food and water from the kitchen. Afterwards, we will go after some magical assistance."

"My question to you, Kellen, is where are we to obtain magical help? I mean, I am skilled in meditation but I'm afraid I only know very little about magical spells and such," Myso asked, worry in his lavender eyes.

"I can answer that for you. We need to visit some old friends of ours from long ago," Narena replied, a smile playing at the corners of her lips.

"And your friends, I assume, are witches?" Myso inquired.

"They sure are. Lorella and Rhoslina are their names. Very fine witches indeed! Kind and thoughtful as they come. I attribute part of Kellen's and my achievements to them."

Narena hugged Kellen around his waist, and the male nymph flushed pink. Even after so many years of marriage, and in the most harrowing of predicaments, Narena's touch never ceased to excite him. Their love for each other was so strong, it was sure to provide in their favor once more, as it did long ago, during the falling.

In a sense, Narena felt as though she was reliving her past adventure, yet this time around she was blessed to have a generation of trust, faith, and love to back her and Kellen's endeavors. And a son, whom she intuitively knew was still alive. He would defeat Rowan and bring the Forest back to its prior normalcy with her and the rest of the group's help.

"I'm heading to the kitchen now," Kellen said, gently pulling away from Narena's grasp. "I'll be back in a moment."

The handsome, aged warrior opened the door slightly and slid his way out as quietly as possible, just as the natural sunlight shining into the home began to wane and fade away. When he got to the kitchen, he grabbed a basket and stuffed it full of what little food he and Narena had left. Then he rolled several water droplets into leaves and placed them atop the food.

He was just about to make his way back to the bedroom when some movement outside of the window caught his attention. Kellen crouched down, peeking just slightly over the windowsill. It was fairly dark outside, but he could make out the form of a horrific being crawling around on the Forest floor in front of his tree home.

The creature resembled a human, and yet was so decrepit and gruesome it looked as though—if it ever were a human—such a long time had passed filled with agony and torture that nothing aside from outward appearance remained of its human nature. The creature cocked its triangular-shaped head around in every direction as it slid across the dirt on its belly, using its elongated arms and fingers to drag itself along.

Kellen held his breath, his heart pounding out of his chest, as he watched the grotesque creature survey the area around his home. Suddenly, he heard a cracking of twigs in the Forest just behind where it slithered. The monster obviously noticed it, too, as it stopped pulling its body along and craned its neck to hear what was approaching.

An innocent-looking male nymph was creeping around in the bushes behind the creature, possibly looking for a place to hide, or berries for food. But for whatever reason, he was out and about in Nymph Kingdom at night, likely unaware or even ignorant of the dangers that the area currently held. The creature saw the nymph before he noticed it, and lashed up from the ground and over the bush, ambushing the helpless being.

Kellen tried to avert his eyes, but found to his dismay that he could not. He saw the creature atop the nymph and tearing at the victim's body, thrashing its large, oddly-shaped head around as it tore the poor nymph to pieces and imbibed his soul.

Despite all his years as a warrior, Kellen shuddered uncontrollably at the horrifying sight. He knew he needed to get back to the bedroom safely, but was frozen in fear as he watched the creature devour the nymph before sliding off into the scarce moonlight. It was only when Kellen could no longer see the monster that he sat on the kitchen floor for a moment, trying to regain his composure. Then, finally he rose up, grabbed the basket, and slunk his way back to the bedroom.

Narena sat next to Basil, stroking his fur while resting her head on his shoulder. Myso sat on the floor next to the window, and was discreetly peeking out of it. Kellen brought the basket of food and water to his wife, who passed everything out amongst the group. The four ate in silence, and only upon completion of the meal did Myso address Kellen.

"Kellen, did you happen to see what happened out the kitchen window earlier?"

"What happened?" Kellen repeated, looking into his wife's worried orange eyes.

"I think if you saw it you know of what I speak. The creature. Did you witness it?" Myso stared at the warrior, who was avoiding eye contact with him.

"I believe so. It was frightening indeed. I just hope it doesn't find itself attracted to our hiding place."

"And if it does, do you know how we combat it?"

"A perfectly placed arrow directly into the third eye should do the trick. It's a negative entity, after all."

"Okay, I wanted to make sure I had it right. It's not every day I get to solicit warrior advice from one of the greatest warriors this Forest has ever seen."

Kellen beamed, but upon realizing what his face was doing immediately pulled his expression back to its usual stoic nature.

"Thank you," he said in a monotone voice. "Let's get some rest now, shall we?"

Narena and Kellen got into their bed, and Basil curled up on a rug on Narena's side. Myso sat cross-legged on the floor by the door and began to meditate. Swirls of white smoke twisted around his body and a sense of calmness filled the room as the four beings drifted off into sleep, resting their tiny bodies for yet another night before they would leave the safety of the nymphs' home and begin their journey once again.

CHAPTER 15

Felix, Eleonora, and Garmon felt around in the darkness of the underground tunnels until they found one another, and clutched together until the burrowing rat approached each of them and tied a piece of stringy fiber around each of their waists. While the small beings' eyes darted around in the complete darkness, the touch of the rat was intensified by the lack of any visual reality. The rat then tied the three fibers to one, which he secured around the base of his tail.

"I will lead you through the tunnels at a pace I deem suitable for your species. I will let you know when it is time to rest. Now, where is it you would like to go?" the rat's voice echoed through the tunnels.

"Nymph Kingdom," Felix replied.

"Nymph Kingdom?! Do you not know how dangerous that area is currently?"

"We are aware of that, Rat," Garmon snapped.

Felix was once again surprised by Garmon's reaction. Now the faery seemed to be defending him, and he wasn't quite sure as to why. Perhaps it was because Garmon just wanted to be disagreeable with someone in general, or that if someone were to be rude to Felix, Garmon felt as though it should be him. But for whatever reason, Garmon was standing behind Felix—as he *should* stand by a member of his own self-proclaimed multi-species army of which he was the leader—and for that, Felix could not complain.

"I'm not saying I won't take you there, I'm just saying that's just about the worst request I've gotten recently. And keep in mind, I come from the darkest part of the Forest," the rat replied, but he had barely finished his sentence before Garmon let out an exasperated groan.

"Time is of the essence, Rat," Garmon sighed.

"That's *Mr. Rat* to you. Now let's go."

The rat took off, tugging on the three beings slightly until they caught up to his pace. The three walked briskly, blind to the world around them, and wondered if they truly could trust this burrowing rat. After all, he was a smooth talker, and came from the darkest part of the Forest, yet he still decided to warn them of the dangers they were about to face. Whether or not his inclination to tell them of the hairy beast by the black oak tree was spawned by the desire for customers or for their own safety was beyond the little beings' comprehension. But whatever the reason, they were in the tunnels now, and all that mattered was protecting the Forest, its harmony, and the ones they loved who dwelt within it—even if that meant one of the faeries would have to surrender their wings in order to accomplish just that.

The rat led them through the blackness of the tunnels for quite some time, but the beings were not able to ascertain any idea of what time of day, or night, they were traveling. All they knew was that they stopped to rest when their little bodies were on the verge of collapse, but the rat did not harbor much sympathy for them. In fact, the burrowing rat even commented that if the little beings were not so prideful as to walk on two legs, they would have a lot less problems maintaining harmony in the Forest. Though Garmon surprisingly held his tongue to this comment, Felix could feel the heat of the male faery's blood boiling with anger simply by standing next to him in the darkness. He was proud of Garmon for keeping his mouth shut for once.

Felix could also sense Eleonora's anxiety over the whole situation. She kept close to him, always clinging to his arm, hand, or even his tunic, and would sometimes squeeze wherever she was grabbing just a little too tightly. Felix would try to calm the faery by rubbing her back, but in the darkness sometimes missed the area he was hoping to rub and touch the faery somewhere inappropriate by accident instead. Eleonora would squeal, and Felix would apologize, but secretly harbor excitement within his own body and revel in the fact that no one was able to see how flushed he likely appeared.

Finally, after a few moments of Eleonora clutching to his hand, the female faery suddenly released her grip and moved closer to the nymph, placing her hand around his waist and slowly trickling her fingers to rest on the small of his back. Felix jumped in surprise, but happily positioned his arm and hand to the same location on the faery's body, and Eleonora responded by clutching her fingers slightly into his stomach.

Felix's mind was nearly spiraling out of control in ecstasy. He wished that he were able to entertain Eleonora's wiles in a different set of circumstances. He promised himself right then and there that if they were to survive the haunting within the Forest, nothing would hold him back from declaring his love for Eleonora through a proposal of marriage.

"How long are we supposed to walk for?" Garmon groaned through the incessant silence.

"I'll let you know when it's time to rest again," the rat grumbled in reply. "For now, we keep walking."

"It shouldn't take too long, Garmon," Eleonora chimed in. "At least we're safe."

"For now," Garmon muttered. "Until we get to Nymph Kingdom and one of us gets our wings chopped off."

Eleonora gasped, and Felix tightened his grip upon her. "Don't worry," he whispered. "Everything will be fine."

Eleonora reached her hand up to brush across Felix's face. "I believe you," she said quietly. "I trust in you more than anybody. Whatever happens, I know I will be fine because I have you by my side."

Felix wished it wasn't so dark, so Eleonora could experience the true magnitude of the love he conveyed with his body language. He opened his mouth to speak, to say aloud what he had felt for so long, but no words would come.

I love you, Eleonora, he thought so fervently within his mind. More than you will ever know.

Felix, Eleonora, and Garmon continued to walk in complete darkness until the burrowing rat finally told them to stop. They had only rested a couple of times since they entered the tunnels, and all three were not only exhausted, but had also found that in the darkness their minds were keen to play tricks on them.

Felix found that the keen intuition he inherited from his mother was running rampant through his mind. Throughout the entire journey through the tunnels, it had been screaming at him not to go to Nymph Kingdom. While at first Felix had ignored the pressing thoughts and kept walking, now that they had stopped he found that his heart was sunk somewhere into his abdomen. He felt as though he may be sick, and knew that if he emerged from the tunnels into Nymph Kingdom that something very bad would happen.

Felix had learned from a very young age from his mother and her salamander friend that intuition was a gift—and an extremely valuable resource, especially in predicaments like the one Felix now found himself in. He was aware that ignoring one's intuition never ended well, so tried to make a point to always pay attention to any pressing thoughts or physical feelings he may be experiencing at any given time.

Once, when he was in warrior training, he was ordered to perform a field test which involved venturing into the outskirts of Troll Kingdom alone, into an uninhabited area of the Forest. He had come across a lost human, a male, who was wandering about the Forest with a domestic pet dog. Felix had heard the man stomping through the crunching leaves ahead of him, and hidden in a bush so he could see who was approaching without being sensed first. He had felt a pit in his stomach, and a sense of worry that left him shaking before his little orange eyes even spotted the human. But the dog, which was black as night with yellow eyes, had sensed Felix, as animals are keener in their sense of detecting presences, and ran over to his bush, barking its head off.

The man came over, and looked the bush up and down, parting back branches frantically in desperation for a meal. But for some reason, the man did not see Felix, which was much in the nymph's favor as the beings of the Forest are forbidden to be looked upon by non-magical human eyes. Felix knew that his intuition had saved him—it had warned him to hide in the bush, which let him blend in and avoid detection.

"All right, I think we've finally made it. Once I push away this rock, you will emerge right on the outskirts of Nymph Kingdom. Now I would like my payment," the rat sneered.

Felix hesitated, and his mind panicked, as he was now sure that Nymph Kingdom was not where they were currently meant to be. He wondered if he could somehow convince the rat to abandon their efforts to emerge into Nymph Kingdom and instead lead them elsewhere—though Felix himself was currently unsure as to where that would be.

Felix cleared his throat. "Garmon, Eleonora, do you trust me?"

"Of course," Eleonora replied instantly.

"Maybe," Garmon mumbled back. "Depends what it's about."

"Just trust me, Garmon, okay? Please?"

"Whatever," Garmon snapped. "If it means I can keep my wings, fine."

"Mr. Rat, I thank you greatly for leading us here. But I am terribly afraid that now I must ask that you now lead us to a different location," Felix said confidently. He held his breath in the darkness and waited for a response from their rat guide.

"What?! You cannot be serious. You owe me payment, and I am supposed to take you elsewhere, simply out of the goodness of my heart?" the rat guffawed. Felix could hear him slap his leg in amusement, similar to how Garmon had when the group had first become aware of the burrowing rat.

"Please, Mr. Rat. I beg of thee," Felix went on. "If you do this, I promise that you will receive faery wings from us. Just lead us to the home of the Elder Triage. Then at least you will be able to offer the witches the faery wings fresh off the back. Surely you would receive higher payment from the witches for the wings being in such lovely condition. Please!"

Felix took a deep breath. He did not know why he had asked to be taken to the Elder Triage, but for some reason couldn't shake the name of the group of the only witches in their Forest out of his mind. But the more he thought about it, the more sense it made to him. He just hoped it would also make sense to the burrowing rat.

"Hmm, I see your point. I would need to travel to the Elders to deliver the wings anyway. Very well! I suppose I will lead you there. But once we arrive, one of the faeries is giving me their wings. Don't try anything funny, as it will not be well-received, and I promise you it will end in one—if not all—of your demises."

The fibers around the waists of the small beings tugged rigorously once again, and they pulled themselves up to follow the rat to their next destination.

Chapter 16

The next morning Myso awoke first, and began to prepare some satchels for the group to carry on their journey to the Elder Triage home. He packed candles, food, water, extra arrows, and spear heads, ensuring that he would be well prepared for any opposition in their way. He woke the rest of his friends, and secured the small blades from their boots to each of their legs as they rubbed their eyes, yawned, and stretched to mentally and physically prepare for their day.

"Is everybody ready? We will need to make good time to arrive at the Elder Triage home before dark," Myso said, opening the door to the bedroom.

"Ready as we'll ever be," Kellen replied.

"Yes, let's get moving," Narena added. "I'm ready to see Lorella and Rhoslina once again."

The four crept downstairs and out of Narena and Kellen's home, down to the creek, and out of Nymph Kingdom. They kept close together, and watched in every direction as they moved. Kellen held on to Narena's hand, as he always did, and would occasionally make eye contact with her and mouth the words that he loved her, something that was comforting enough to ease Narena's tension, and had worked for many years.

Basil and Myso walked together, and despite the recent harrowing occurrences, the two kept their spirits high by joking around with one another and making goofy faces in each others' directions. Kellen and Narena did not seem to mind in the slightest, as the two were causing no harm and staying fairly quiet. The married couple were firm believers that whatever one needed to do in order to calm themselves down during a difficult situation was good enough for them, so long as it didn't impede the mood of anyone else. Myso found this to be a welcomed response—as Garmon would surely act sour if he were in Kellen and Narena's position—and spent as much time as he could bonding further with his good friend. As a warrior, Myso was unsure as to how much longer he would be so blessed as to be with his very best friend, so wanted to make the most of any silliness he could before they were thrust into an inevitable situation where silliness would no longer be an option.

The four walked for quite some time until they stopped to rest upon a fallen log along the banks of the creek. They stayed vigilant, but they felt comfortable enough to quietly talk amongst each other as they rested their bodies and munched on some bread. The four were just preparing themselves to leave when the water in the creek in front of them stirred, and grayish flesh began to slowly emerge from the surface.

Two webbed hands grabbed the dirt of the bank, and pulled a bipedal body out of the creek, dragging itself by wriggling its belly. A reflective pool of water sloshing about in the hollow of the creature's head caught the sunlight, and the group barely had time to gasp when the creature stood upright before them, blocking the sunlight with its thick, wide head. The creature bared down upon them, mocking them silently with a gaping, frog-like grin.

"Gorgon!" Kellen cried. "I knew we shouldn't have stopped here!"

"It's a kalpie. Don't move," Myso hissed. His body began to puff up, making him almost as large as the creature, but not quite as tall.

Kellen shoved Narena behind him and readied his bow. Basil stood next to Myso, backwards and standing on his front legs. Narena unsheathed her blade and Myso readied his spear.

"Do not come any closer, Kalpie, or the next move will be your last!" Kellen shouted. "I have no qualms about killing you, as I have slain your kind many, many times before!"

"As I have with your kind as well, Nymph," the kalpie retorted.

"Don't listen to him," Narena hissed. "He's trying to get to you."

Narena, of course, was referring to the ruthless murder of Kellen's mother by a kalpie, when Kellen was just a young lad. This incident had prompted the kalpies to be pushed out of the populated Forest area, and into the unincorporated land. But since the current haunting was causing all the established protective barriers of the Forest's realms to weaken, the few remaining kalpies were now once again free to wreak havoc wherever they pleased.

"What are you doing in this part of the Forest, Kalpie?" Myso inquired, speaking sternly and keeping his spear at the ready.

"There are no longer barriers. I can move freely about the Forest at my will—all negative entities and beings can, now. There are no rules anymore!"

The kalpie's gaping mouth waggled around as it spoke, and the water atop its head sloshed around, a few drops leaping from the pool as if trying to escape the hollow of the creature's brain. The creature laughed maniacally, prompting Kellen to release an arrow, which grazed the upper left side of the kalpie's lip. The kalpie flinched, and more water sloshed out of its head.

It held up its hand to the wound, and inspected its hand before licking it and rubbing the wound once more. Then the kalpie stormed toward the group, and Myso ran back at it, slicing through its right arm with his spear. More water fell out of the kalpie's head, but the troll could see there was still a substantial amount of water still in the hole.

Kellen released another arrow, which stuck in the kalpie's shoulder, while Basil sprayed musk into the creature's face. The kalpie stumbled back, and tripped over a protruding rock on the bank of the creek, falling on its rear end and losing about half of the remaining pool of water. Narena saw her opportunity and rushed past Kellen, providing one good, strong shove. The kalpie tumbled onto its side and emptied what was left of the pool of water in its head into the mud of the bank. The kalpie wailed, and dragged itself into the creek, disappearing from view beneath the surface.

"Is everybody all right?" Myso asked, and the two nymphs and skunk nodded.

"We'd better keep moving. Once the kalpie replenishes the water in its head it can emerge again," Kellen said.

So the four ventured off, keeping a further distance away from the creek than they had before. They soon found a deer trail heading in the direction they were traveling, so they began to follow it, all the more alert than they were before their kalpie ordeal, and all unknowing of what else was to come.

"Why don't we just ask the Yew for help?" Basil spoke up after the group had walked for some time. "Isn't that how you two stopped the falling?"

"It's not likely the Yew could do much for us in this situation," Narena replied. "Our foe was once of flesh and blood, not a Higher Spirit like Labete. The Yew was needed in the falling because only a Higher Spirit can destroy another Higher Spirit—or an Under Spirit, for that matter, since Agrimon was fused with Labete."

"Since Rowan was once a being of light, he must henceforth be destroyed by a being of light," Kellen added. "I know I'd be happy to make that happen, but destiny seems to dictate that it should be my son. That's the next best scenario." He winked at his wife, who beamed in return.

"We have to keep the Forest's balance," Myso said. "I'd always heard that growing up, but now it makes sense more than ever. It's imperative to the Forest's survival."

"Exactly," Narena said. "But we as beings of light can ask for a little help, which is exactly what we are doing now!"

When they finally reached the Elder Triage tree home, Narena couldn't help but run to the front door and pound on it rapidly in the tune of a well-known nymph folk song. She had not seen the witches Lorella and Rhoslina since the falling, and she was eager to reconnect with her old friends. Heavy footsteps approached the door and the tall, thin man with a long, gray beard that the beings had met just days earlier answered.

"Why hello there, little beings! What can I do for you?" the man said, smiling. He seemed oddly unfazed by all the harrowing occurrences in the Forest.

The man had deep, sea-foam green eyes and quite a large nose, which curled over his moist, plump upper lip as if preparing to dive from his face to the ground below. The man smacked his lips and rubbed his hands together before bending down and using his hand to scoot the four small beings into the home, muttering that it was safer for them to speak inside.

"Are Lorella and Rhoslina here?" Narena asked as soon as the front door was shut and locked behind them.

"I'm afraid not, little one. Unfortunately, you just missed them. They left to take care of some matters in the human world," the man replied, crouching down to speak on the nymph's level.

"What could possibly be more important than the current plight of our Forest?"

Narena couldn't help the tears that began to swell in her orange eyes. She felt disappointed that the two humans she once considered her friends and allies would take off during such a crucial time.

"Do not fret, my dear. The witches left with the purpose of helping the Forest. I cannot say what it is they are doing, but I can assure you that it is all for the good of all beings. They will be back tomorrow—that is, if they accomplish what it is they hope to."

"So why are you at their home, then?" Kellen asked.

"I was visiting before all the terrible things began to happen. Now I am merely watching their home for them while they are away. I'm Magus."

"Are you a wizard?" Narena asked.

"Yes. I have ventured here from a faraway land because I heard the Elder Triage was in need of a third. I am skilled in the art of exorcisms, but I dabble in potion concocting as well."

"Then you would be a perfect match for the Elders! Odila knew about potions and Nessaba knew about exorcising spirits and things of that nature. Did you know of them?" Narena's excitement over meeting Magus was beginning to soften her feelings of disappointment over Lorella and Rhoslina's absence. She noticed that Magus was motioning for her to be lifted up onto the arm of a soft, purple velvet sitting chair, so she obliged, and spoke to the wizard as he gently sat down next to her.

"I did, as a matter of fact. Terrible tragedies, both of them. I can only hope I can live up to the witches that came before me in this Forest. Though I have not resided here long, I have fallen in love with this land and wish to live here. If the Elders will have me, that is." Magus chuckled and leaned back in the sitting chair.

Narena watched him for a moment, then looked down at her husband and friends, who were standing on the ground staring back up at them.

"Magus, we are very pleased to meet you indeed, but I'm afraid we visit with a purpose. Nymph Kingdom is in turmoil, and it's not long before the other kingdoms will be overrun as well, if they haven't been already," Kellen said fervently up at the wizard, who promptly reached down, picked him up, and set him down next to his wife.

Then Magus grabbed Myso and Basil and lifted them up to sit upon his lap. Basil curled up into a ball and perked up his ears to hear the conversation, while Myso sat cross-legged upon the wizard's knee.

"I am painfully aware of this fact. It's true, barriers have been broken, and the Forest is on the verge of being completely and hopelessly haunted. And if Lorella's divination is correct—and I assume it is, as you four small beings stand before me now—I am to help you by exorcising the negative entities from the underworld out of the Forest, and close the barriers back to normal."

Magus smiled at the little beings, and Kellen put his arm around Narena. Both were happy that the wizard knew what they needed from him, since they'd known that they needed magical help, but not the specifics of their request.

"How can we help? What is it you need from us?" Myso finally spoke up to the large, bearded face in front of him.

"First off, I would like to know your names. And I would like to know what you've experienced in Nymph Kingdom. It will help me become more familiar with what I am up against."

"I am Myso, this is Basil, and Kellen and Narena are the two nymphs at your side. We are warriors of the Forest."

"Except me!" Narena pointed out, something she was prone to do as she was not trained as a warrior, and found no reason to deceive anyone into thinking she was.

"Kellen and Narena! I've heard much about you. Consider me honored to exist in your presence." Magus beamed at the nymphs.

The four small beings then took turns explaining every minute detail of their recent experiences, making sure to include Felix and the faeries' disappearance, and Basil's dream of Sator's directions. The wizard listened intently with wide eyes, nodding his head occasionally or stroking his beard. When they had finished, Magus sat silently for a moment, then reached into his pocket and pulled out a pipe, which he lit and puffed on as he absorbed all the information.

"That is quite the tale indeed! So we must take extra care to ensure that your son and his friends are able to make it to Rowan unopposed. The easier we can make it for them, the better. The only problem that you may find with my assistance is that in order to perform the exorcism spell required to close the barriers and send the negative entities back to the underworld, I will need a rare ingredient that may offend your nature."

The wizard finished his pipe, tapped it out into a bowl on the table next to his chair, and placed the pipe down next to it.

"What ingredient might that be?" Myso asked, his voice slightly shaky.

"And how is it offensive to us?" Kellen chimed in.

"Not to any of you beings. It is found on the body of faeries, which, luckily for you, none of you are."

"And what body part is that?" Myso sounded somewhat exasperated at the conversation.

"Wings."

"Oh, no, why would a spell ever require the need for faery wings?" Narena exclaimed. Though she was not a faery herself, she was extremely empathetic to sufferings of other species. She was very intuitive as well, and knew once Magus said they would need faery wings that they would be coming from either Eleonora or Garmon once they found them. Secretly she hoped they would be from Garmon, as she saw the male faery as a soul in desperate need of some life lessons about sympathy, whether he was aware of it or not. But either way, Narena couldn't help but feel sorry for whatever faery was fated to donate the set of wings needed for their spell, which was imperative to the Forest's survival.

"I do not decide the ingredients for such spells, unfortunately. They are dictated by ancient magic," the wizard replied, but his eyes seemed to share Narena's sentiment.

"Well, since there are no faeries here, that would mean we would need to somehow locate my son and his comrades, bring them here, and convince one of the faeries to surrender their wings for this spell. Am I correct?" Kellen said. He didn't intend to sound as forceful as he did, but time was of the essence, and if he had learned anything from his ordeal in the falling, it was that the longer they waited, the more damage the darkness would do.

"You are correct. Now, I would suggest performing a divination to see where your son and his friends are. It's unfortunate that Lorella is not here to help, but I think I can get by with what little knowledge I have on the matter."

The wizard made some quick preparations for the divination, then motioned for the group to sit around the witches' crystal ball. Then he lit a mixture of sweet-smelling herbs and spoke a brief, incomprehensible incantation aloud, resonant sounds and babbling words.

"Felix, Eleonora, and Garmon," Magus called out as he waved his hands around the ball. "Show us your location. So shall it be!"

The wizard's voice changed, and the crystal began to experience a swirling of glittery white smoke, which moiled around until a full picture began to come into view. It was complete blackness, and yet the beings could barely make out the silhouettes of four beings moving about in the darkness.

Narena could immediately see that one of the outlines was her son, and then was relieved when she perceived that he was indeed still accompanied by two faeries. In front of them, however, was the form of a large rat, and though Narena generally loved all animals, even rats, she couldn't ignore the strange feeling the vision gave her.

After a moment of watching the blackened image of the small travelers, the white smoke began to swirl around the crystal once more, engulfing the image and pulling it away from view.

"Well, I guess we now have a better idea than we did before," Magus said, and leaned over to stroke the crystal, which he found was hot to the touch.

Magus tickled his fingers across the ball, as he was very easily amused, and the heat of a crystal after a divination never ceased to delight him. He was a fun-loving wizard, one who might be described as silly, and despite his penchant for magic had been known to play a practical joke or two—in a different time, when the matters he was engaged in weren't as pressing as they were now. But Magus could not help but try to keep his happiness levels high, even in difficult times, using humor as a way of helping him deal with various negative situations he came across in his existence.

"So where do we think they are?" Myso inquired as he watched the wizard with wide eyes, hoping that the magical human could decipher the location of his friends.

"I'd say they're either underground or in a cave. That's my best guess," the wizard replied.

"If they are in a cave, I doubt they will be able to make it back in time to stop Rowan from destroying the Forest any further. And if he is set on destroying the Higher Spirits, then we would really need to progress in our quest to stop him," Myso said, furrowing his brow and exchanging a glance with Basil. Trolls have wrinkly foreheads in general, but for one to look upset or angry really amplifies the lines of the face. Myso looked generations older simply by imparting this look upon his skunk friend. Narena glanced at the two of them, then her husband, and closed her eyes, concentrating harder than she had in years.

Hawthorne, she thought fervently within her mind. I am not yet as strong of a sage as you once were. I feel that Felix is not in a cave, so he must be underground, right?

Silly Narena, Hawthorne's indisputable voice resounded a reply within her thoughts. You know as well as I do that you know the answer to that. Stop questioning yourself! You're a sage now, just as strong as I was. Trust yourself.

Narena eyes burst open. "They're underground," she said earnestly, looking to her husband, who glanced back at her with tender eyes and nodded in approval.

"How do you know?" Magus asked.

"I know my son. I can feel where he is. He's coming to us, getting closer with each step. We need not do anything more, just wait for them to arrive," Narena said strongly and confidently. All in the room did not find it necessary to question her.

Her mother's intuition was spot on, and she knew deep in her heart that she was correct in her seemingly random assumptions. She just hoped that once her son and the faeries got to the Elder Triage home, they would then have a plan for breaking the news about the need for faery wings. Hopefully, Garmon would perform his duties as a leader and surrender his. If not willingly, then they would have no choice but to do it forcefully.

Chapter 17

Felix, Eleonora, and Garmon had walked for an extended length of time unrealized by the passing of light of day to darkness of night—or perhaps the other way around. When the burrowing rat finally stopped, they eagerly sat down for a much needed rest.

"Rest up, because we still have quite a ways to go. The next time we stop, we will be near the Elder Triage tree. So you better start deciding who will give me their wings when we arrive," the rat said. The sound of him licking his body followed; presumably he was bathing himself to enhance his appearance before reaching the home of the witches.

"Why must the wings be cut off prior to reaching the witches?" Felix asked. "Would we not be permitted to keep the wings at least until we enter the home to sell them?"

"Absolutely not. I want the wings in my possession when we knock upon the door. The witches might feel bad for the faery, and not accept them if they are still attached. They must be cut off prior," the rat replied curtly.

Felix exhaled deeply. He knew the rat was right. The witches were kind, despite any bad reputation the inhabitants of the Forest may have bestowed upon them. Felix knew from stories his parents shared with him that the witches were generally eager to help, and only wanted good to come of the Forest. The witches surely would not approve of pulling the wings right off a faery's back, even if they truly did intend to use them for the purpose of completing a spell.

"I'm glad we aren't able to see each other," Garmon spoke through Felix's thoughts. "Otherwise I'd swear that you two were looking at me to donate my wings."

"We weren't," Felix practically snapped back. "But if you'd care to volunteer, you'd make this decision a lot easier on all of us."

"As the leader of a warrior army, I must argue that I need my wings in order to perform my duties," Garmon replied.

"But by that same token, couldn't Eleonora argue the same thing?" Felix said, feeling himself getting angrier and angrier at Garmon's lack of responsibility as their leader. "I could even venture to say, that as the leader you *should* be the one to give up your wings!"

"A female without wings is looked upon with sympathy and condolence. A male without wings is seen as weak."

"And to think I was foolish enough to believe you actually had feelings for Eleonora," Felix said. "You are a disappointment to your position."

"You're the disappointment!" Garmon yelled. "Look at all your parents have done! What have you done for this Forest, Felix, besides harass me incessantly and bring misfortune on our army?"

"At least I would be noble enough of a being to give my wings to save a lady's!"

"Well, you don't have wings. So you wouldn't understand how important they are."

"I've done just fine my whole life without wings, thank you very much."

"Stop it!" Eleonora cried out. "Both of you, please! Just stop!"

The tunnel was silent, except for the sound of the rat snickering to himself in the background as he groomed his fur.

"I'm just trying to help you, Eleonora," Felix said quietly. "You weren't defending yourself, so..."

"I don't need to," Eleonora replied frankly. "I will give my wings."

"No, Eleonora," Felix pleaded. "Forest law dictates that if a sacrifice is ever to be made in the name of the Forest, he or she of the highest status should be the one to do it."

"If she wills her right to be the one of sacrifice, I cannot disagree," Garmon chimed in. "As a leader, I am required to perform the duties best suited for survival. I need my wings."

"You really are a piece of work, Garmon," Felix muttered. "You don't love Eleonora. You don't even know what love is."

"How would you know?" Garmon snapped. "I'll have you know I am very well-versed in the language of love!"

"You wouldn't know what love was if it speared you through the heart!" Felix cried.

"But Felix," Eleonora broke in, her voice shaky. "It is because of love that I volunteer to sacrifice my wings!"

Felix froze in place. He opened his mouth, but no words would come. His whole body was flushed with heat, and his heart pounded so hard it nearly shot out of his chest.

"What do you mean?" Felix whispered, barely able to speak.

"Without my wings, I'd be a nymph, like you. And if we survive this haunting, I do not wish to return to Faery Kingdom, anyway. Ever. I will live out my days in Troll Kingdom if I have to. Or Nymph Kingdom, if you'll have me. I don't care, as long as you are by my side."

"Oh, Eleonora!"

Felix found the faery in the darkness and wrapped his arms around her, squeezing her soft body as tightly as he could. He wished he would never have to release his grip upon her, and was unable to control the tears that began to stream down his face, falling into her hair. He breathed in her scent deeply, his memory locking away the smell of honeysuckle mixed with lavender and rosemary. He never wanted the moment to end.

"Time's up. Let's get moving again."

The rat's voice pained Felix's ears, yet he readied himself to move again, still clutching Eleonora, and began to walk. Whether or not Garmon was still even tied to the rat's tail was irrelevant to Felix. He vowed in his mind to never give the male faery the benefit of his kindness ever again.

"Garmon, you are a horrible being," Felix hissed into the silence of the underground tunnels. He felt Eleonora cringe beside him, and for a brief moment her hand trembled a bit.

"Must I explain my reasoning again, Felix?" Garmon sighed.

"Perhaps you should, as I still cease to comprehend it."

"Your lack of comprehension is just another significant difference between faeries and nymphs. You can't understand why I need my wings, simple as that."

"Oh, your wings! It's always about the wings, isn't it? Wings are why faeries think they're superior to nymphs, and why your kind feel the need to discriminate against us. Can you not accept that nymphs are perfectly happy the way we are, without the need for wings? I think it's the wings that actually make you insane, Garmon. You're going to need to grow up and take responsibility for your position at some point."

"It is *you*, Felix, that needs to grow up. And you'd do best not to speak to me in such a manner again. I may not be superior to you in the eyes of the Higher Spirits, but I am certainly so in regards to the Troll Kingdom army."

"Please, you two, that's enough. I am volunteering my wings and that is that. And as recognition for doing so, I'd like to request that you two knock it off. I'm so tired of hearing you two argue. You're both different, I get it. And frankly, I'm tired of hearing about it."

"Yeah. Shut it or I'll abandon you all right here and now," the rat snapped.

The three small beings and the burrowing rat traveled for a while, completely engulfed in an awkward silence. It was only when the nymph and faeries' feet were beginning to grow sore once again that the rat stopped.

"All right, we're right outside the Elder Triage home. Time for the wings," the rat sneered.

"Are we to remove the wings here, in the darkness?" Felix asked.

"Ah, well I suppose that wouldn't work. Let's exit the tunnels, and find a safe hiding spot where I can gnaw off the wings privately before approaching the witches."

The sound of rock scraping through dirt filled the little beings ears, and shortly after that light began to peek its way into the darkness. Then the rock moved completely, and the three beings were nearly blinded by the sunlight as it scorched into the tunnels. After a short pause to allow their little eyes to adjust, the nymph and faeries followed the rat out of the exit hole and into the Forest. The Elder Triage tree was in view, yet the rat led the three into a blackberry bush nearby.

"We decided it would be the female, yes?" the rat confirmed, and licked his tongue over his incisors.

"Yes," Eleonora said quietly, her face wholly disconnected from the current situation.

"Very well. Stand with your back to me, so I can get a good angle. This is not an easy task, you know," the rat said.

"Believe me, we are well aware of its torment of you," Garmon said sarcastically, and Felix shot him an angry glare. But knowing how anxious Eleonora must feel, Felix held his tongue. Snapping at Garmon would surely not help the situation.

"This might hurt a little," the rat muttered, and Felix saw Eleonora's face cringe in pain.

"Ow, it really hurts!" she wailed, and Felix grabbed her hand and held it tightly.

He watched as Eleonora's left wing began to hang loosely from her back, then finally fell to the ground, swaying back and forth as it drifted downward, until it finally slid along the dirt and stopped. The rat repeated his method on the right wing, and Eleonora cried out in pain as the second wing followed the first.

Once the right wing had landed silently on the ground, Felix ripped his tunic off and forcefully pressed the fabric into Eleonora's back, holding off the bleeding from where the wings had been sliced off. Elenora wept softly, shaking slightly, and covered her eyes with her hands. Garmon stood off to the side, watching with wide eyes, mouth agape, but saying nothing.

The burrowing rat picked up the two wings and motioned for the three to follow him over to the Elder Triage home. Eleonora was still sobbing, though trying to hide it, and Felix kept his tunic and hand firmly planted on her back wound.

"Everything is going to be all right," Felix whispered, his face close to her ear. "You are an amazing being for doing this. I love you more than anything on the earth."

"I do not regret what I have done," she replied softly. "But I think I might need to lie down for a bit."

"I'm sure the witches will make you very comfortable," Felix replied.

Eleonora cracked a tiny smile at the nymph, but did not say a word back to him, merely nodding and every once in awhile turning to glance at him, her tearful teal eyes looking into his sparkling orange ones.

Though her kind considered themselves blessed, Eleonora had always secretly held an admiration for her wingless brethren, the nymphs. They were so carefree, thoughtful of others, kind, and though sometimes oblivious, were almost always backed by good intentions.

Eleonora did not know that many nymphs in general, as her station in Troll Kingdom provided her the pleasure of having the opportunity to get to know just one, but if Felix was any form of example of the nature of nymphs then that alone was good enough for her. Plus, Eleonora was never really attached to her wings, and Felix had a way of inspiring her to believe that walking on the earth was not something to ever be ashamed of. And if cutting her wings off could save her from the unwanted and unwarranted advances of Garmon, well, that was just an added bonus.

The burrowing rat knocked impatiently on the Elder Triage door. "Hello! Magic ingredient service here! Anybody home?"

Silence.

"Maybe nobody is home," Garmon commented.

"They sure as Gorgon better be," the rat complained.

After a few more moments of the rat pounding impatiently upon the door, it finally opened, and the tall, thin silhouette of Magus the wizard appeared before them. The rat's demeanor suddenly changed.

"Well, hello there, good sir! I have a proposition for you. What would you say, if I told you, that I had freshly cut faery wings, available for purchase at the deal of a lifetime?"

The rat grinned a toothy smile, and the wizard glanced down at him, looking slightly confused as he noticed Felix and Eleonora standing behind the rat.

"Why don't you all come inside? It's much safer in here," Magus replied, and moved aside so the four beings could enter. Once all four were inside, Magus shut and locked the door behind them.

"Felix?!" Narena had been sitting on a rug next to the velvet chair, cuddling with Basil as Kellen and Myso sat on the chair, talking amongst themselves.

"Mother?! Father?! And Myso, and Basil!"

Felix couldn't hide his excitement at seeing his friends, but didn't want to release his pressure from Eleonora's wound, so allowed his mother, father, and friends to approach him so he could embrace them while still holding off Eleonora's bleeding back.

"Eleonora! What happened to you?" Narena asked. "Are you all right?"

"Wait, are those your wings?" Myso broke in, looking from the rat's grubby hands to the wings that were grasped within them, then to Eleonora's wound.

"Yes. I volunteered to sell them to the rat as payment for guiding us safely through the underground tunnels of the Forest," Eleonora replied.

"I thought that the being of the highest status was required to make a sacrifice when one is necessary for survival," Kellen spoke up, furrowing his brow at Garmon.

"I thought so, too," Felix added. "But apparently those rules don't apply when a male faery is the leader and needs them so others don't perceive him as weak."

"Hmm," Kellen said, now raising both eyebrows.

"It's okay, everyone," Eleonora interjected. "Really, I'm okay with this. Can we please just drop it?"

"Sure, my dear," Narena said, then turned her attention to Kellen. "Honey, why don't you use some of your healing abilities on Eleonora's back wound?"

"Sure, I can do that. Come over here, Eleonora," Kellen said.

Kellen instructed the faery to lie face down on the rug, while he rigorously rubbed his two hands together, generating heat to radiate through the lesion. Then he drifted his hands delicately over and across the whole width of the wound, and after a few short moments her back had already begun to look as though it were mostly back to normal.

"I think that's all I can do," Kellen said, motioning for Eleonora that she could get up. "The rest of it will heal on its own."

"Thank you, Kellen," the female faery replied with a grin. "It feels better already."

The burrowing rat impatiently cleared his throat as loudly as he could, drawing Magus's attention to him.

"Ah yes, the wings. What would you like for them, sir?" the wizard asked in a calm voice.

"If possible, I would like to trade them for several days worth of food and water in a satchel, if you please. I plan on fleeing this Forest, now that it has erupted in such turmoil. My grandfather spoke of the falling, but I imagine this plight is probably much worse. I cannot stand to live here anymore," the rat replied.

"Where do you intend to go?" Narena asked, not surprisingly, as she was one to always address an animal in her presence.

"Where the humans dwell. I hear there is endless food, all the food one could dream of."

"Like you need any more food!" Garmon said under his breath.

"If that is what you want, so shall it be. I'll be right back," the wizard said.

Magus sauntered into the kitchen, and all the small beings could hear him rustling around for a few moments, until he returned with a nymph-sized satchel. He handed the satchel to the rat, and the rat handed the wings to Magus. The rat opened it, surveyed his goods, then gave each being a nod as Magus opened the door to let him out. The rat looked around, then darted back to the entrance to his tunnels. And that was the last the group ever saw of him.

CHAPTER 18

nce the burrowing rat had gone, the beings replenished themselves and caught up on everything that had happened the last few days. Felix put on a new tunic that he had brought along in his satchel, while his mother rushed Eleonora to a bedroom to help her fashion a bandage from Felix's old tunic that wrapped tightly around her midsection to protect the still-sensitive, mostly-healed wound on her back.

"How are you doing?" Narena asked, a kind look upon her face. "Did the healing help with the pain?"

"Actually, yes," Eleonora replied, smiling. "You have quite the husband, Narena. You're very lucky. I see a lot of him in Felix."

"Yes," Narena beamed. "Whomever is fortunate enough to become my son's wife will be a very cherished and protected being. And I shouldn't say this, but--" she paused and gazed at the faery for a moment, "you know he fancies you, right?"

"I know," Eleonora said. "I fancy him too."

"Is that why you surrendered your wings? To be with him?"

"I can't imagine not being with him," Elenora replied. "He's everything to me. I wish I could be more like him, more brave, more giving. Plus, I've always admired the nymphs. You are all so kindhearted and generous with your love. And you ask for nothing in return. Faeries are not all like that. I never felt like I belonged with them. Now, with my wings gone, I feel strangely rejuvenated. Like I became what I was always meant to be. I'm happy with my decision."

Narena's eyes uncontrollably filled with tears. "Well, you know, Eleonora, you have our blessing. I'd love nothing more than to have you as a daughter-in-law. Even if it means my son would be a flutterbum," she joked. "But don't worry, my brother is one, too."

"And I would be honored to be that daughter-in-law," Eleonora said, grinning. "What's a flutterbum?"

Narena laughed. "Oh, it's nothing, darling. Just some lingo from back when I was your age. I guess the young folk don't use that term anymore. Let's head back to the living room, shall we?"

The two went back to the rest of the group, and Magus immediately called for everyone to gather around him. So the nymphs, faeries, troll, skunk, and wizard gathered in the sitting room where the divination had been performed and made themselves comfortable. Narena and Kellen sat with their son, Felix, who kept Eleonora close by his side. Myso and Basil sat together, joking around quietly to each other as they normally did. Only Garmon kept to himself, off to the side of the velvet chair. Magus sat down in the chair, sighed loudly, and began to speak to the small beings before him.

"My little friends, the time has come for us to decide what is to be done next. I now have everything at my fingertips necessary to perform the exorcism spell which would close the barriers of the Forest once more, and shut the doorway to the underworld. I can perform this spell alone. I will not need your assistance with that. However, I do need one thing from you before I can properly perform the spell."

The wizard looked from each individual to the next, holding eye contact for a moment before moving on. All eyes were locked on him.

"What do you need, Magus?" Narena replied.

"Rowan must be destroyed and his body thrown into the doorway. If you cannot finish him off yourself, you must somehow get him through the doorway and back into the underworld. It's imperative that he is in the underworld when the doorway is actually closed. Rowan is the opener of the doorway, which makes him the key to closing it. As long as he exists in this Forest, there is no way I can make everything go back to normal—or as close as I can to normal." The wizard spoke sternly, which was out of the ordinary for him, but he needed to get his point across.

Everyone nodded in agreement. All had been aware that at some point it would come to this, and no one—not even Kellen, who was once a friend to Rowan—seemed to have a problem with the task at hand.

"We should leave soon, so Magus can begin the preparations for his spell. I do not relish the fact that we will be traveling through the night, but it's something we absolutely have to do. Every moment we have to stop this haunting counts," Kellen said in a low voice, looking directly at his son.

"I will perform a divination to determine exactly when I should begin my spell," Magus explained. "Remember, you must destroy any entity that emerges from the underworld before the doorway can be closed. That, or somehow get those entities to go back through the doorway before I close it. Destroying them is probably your easiest option. That includes Rowan. But he must be defeated last. Then I can shut the doorway the proper way, adding a protective blockage cleansing so this doesn't happen again."

"Prepare to leave, everyone. Brandish whatever weapon you're able to. Narena and Eleonora, make sure you grab some satchels of supplies," Garmon boomed at everyone.

"Because females are only capable of providing supplies to our quest?" Kellen asked sarcastically, glaring at the male faery.

"Females are good for lots of things," Garmon snapped back. "One of them just happens to be collecting resources."

"I'll have you know that my wife played in integral role in defeating Labete and ending the falling," Kellen scolded. "Had she not, you might not even be around today to speak so rudely to her. I'll let your insolence pass this time. Speak ill of my wife—or any females for that matter—again, and you will surely see a side of me that, trust me, you'll wish you hadn't."

Garmon stared at Kellen for a moment, shocked. "Okay, okay," he said. "No need to get your undergarments in a twist."

"Next rule," Kellen went on, "no speaking of my undergarments either. In fact, unless it's directly related to our quest, don't talk to me or my wife at all."

"That sounds good to me," Garmon quipped. "Can we go now, everyone?"

"The negative energy from the haunting is affecting us," Magus announced, nodding at Kellen and Garmon. "We must be aware of these feelings, and not turn on each other. Remember this, my little beings—the anger is not entirely your own. Always remember to love."

Kellen approached his son and delicately handed him an extra bow and several arrows that he had stuffed in a satchel before leaving his home with his wife, Myso, and Basil.

"Thank you, Father," Felix replied.

"It is my pleasure, son. I am quite proud of you, you know," Kellen said. "You should be proud of yourself, too. You're a true warrior."

"I guess I've always known that, but it's great to hear you say it aloud," Felix replied, hugging his father.

"Of course, you are aware that I have always been proud of you, Felix," Kellen said. "I apologize if I haven't shown it as much as I should have. That's something my father did to me, and I swore to myself that I wouldn't treat you that way."

"I'm honored to be your son," was all Felix could reply.

"Now, are you ready for what lies ahead?"

"You mean the unknown? Ready as I'll ever be, I suppose!"

Felix watched his father chuckle at his words, experiencing a happiness not yet known to him in his adult life. Now, more than ever, he felt as though he was where he was meant to be. Everything in his life that he had questioned before was now slowly falling into place. Perhaps it was the adventure that he had always longed for that was doing so.

Once everyone was ready and had bid their goodbyes to Magus, the wizard opened the door for them and each individual darted out of the Elder Triage tree home and into the shelter of the blackberry bush nearby—the very same bush in which Eleonora had been stripped of her wings.

The multi-species army of Troll Kingdom was together once more, about to embark on likely the most important battle of their lives. But this time, they were blessed enough to have been joined by two of the most accomplished warriors of the Forest in their own right, Narena and Kellen. And though Narena never considered herself a true warrior, she was still a pinnacle figure in ending the falling in the Forest so many years ago. Though she was much older than she'd been during her first ordeal, Narena felt more prepared and ready for the task in question. The love in her heart and soul had benefited her in her first adventure, and her faith in that was so strong that she knew it gave her additional power.

Myso snapped off some particularly thick, long, and sharply pointed thorns from the blackberry bush and stuck them in one of the satchels. Then the army all collectively took a deep breath and crawled out of the thick bush, with Garmon taking the lead and Kellen holding up the rear. The army marched away from the Elder Triage home and into the Forest, heading back towards Nymph Kingdom.

Chapter 19

owan was just beginning to notice, in all his selfishness, that his main henchman, Caul, had been missing for quite some time. Possibly days, even, Rowan was realizing, as the last time he'd seen the goblin was when he was taking the troll back to the dungeon.

Rowan's consciousness remained within his rotting former-nymph body, yet his mind he sometimes found to be elsewhere. He could only assume that he had been sitting on the throne; his flesh melting and decomposing into his skeleton, daydreaming, and perusing *The Book of the Dead*. He had planned his revenge for days—thinking of every possible detail, however minute. In all his meticulousness, he must have lost track of time. The underworld had provided him no sense of time or space for a whole generation, and being in a realm that did was something he was still getting used to.

Rowan attributed his own personal falling as a nymph to the fact that Labete, a former Higher Spirit possessed by his counterpart Agrimon, had caused his demise by sending a slew of insects to destroy a sector of the Nymph Army. He blamed Labete for his transformation, though his embrace of the darkness is what truly sealed his fate. But Rowan was prideful, and like his father, always had been, so admitting to himself that he was partially responsible for his outcome was something he was certainly not inclined to do.

Rowan slid his waste of a body off the throne and sauntered over to the doorway to the underworld. He peeked down at the darkness below, which was still emitting a red light that would glow brightly then wane, forming a pattern that was too complicated for the former nymph to be aware of. He walked over to the entrance to the throne room and called out for a goblin to come to him. A short, stocky wretch appeared.

"What can I do for you, master?" the goblin hissed.

"Where is Caul?" Rowan inquired, his sunken, yellowed-blue eyes baring into the goblin's soul.

"I do not know. I have not seen him for quite some time, so I assumed that he was out in the Forest wreaking havoc like the rest of us. Do you not know of his whereabouts?"

"No. Please go down to the dungeon and make sure that our prisoners are still confined."

The goblin nodded at Rowan's request and made his way down the hallway and down the stairs. Several moments later, he emerged, and if there were any color in his face to begin with, it had sunk into the pit of his belly.

"My liege, I'm afraid that the prisoners are all gone. Caul's body lies at the bottom of the steps. He is dead, my king."

The goblin bowed and lowered his eyes, and for a moment Rowan felt a hint of sympathy for the creature who submitted before him. But as quick as that feeling came, it was gone, and Rowan shrieked in anger.

"It was that troll! Get to the Forest and find him! Bring his body to me, dead or alive! Destroy anyone who attempts to aid him!"

Rowan found himself heaving in all his frustration as the goblin scuttled out of the palace. As soon as the goblin was out of sight, Rowan howled in vexation. He was livid. Being easily angered was not a trait of Rowan's that entirely stemmed from his time spent in the underworld. Rowan had always been fairly difficult, as he had the tendency to feel as though any problem that affected him was always the fault of someone else. He'd never been one to take responsibility for his actions either, which was certainly exacerbated by the fact that he was the son and rightful heir to the Nymph King throne.

It was hard to believe that, at one point, Rowan could have been considered a good friend of a nymph who was essentially his polar opposite—Kellen. But the two had found an odd, yet satisfactory friendship in one another during their time spent together in warrior training, and, of course, growing up at the palace together. Theirs was a friendship that had not withstood the test of time, or death. But secretly—though he would never admit to such a thought—Rowan admired Kellen: his ability to remain calm during times of distress, and the fact that he was always willing and able to take responsibility for not just himself, but for others as well. And Kellen was the mysterious type of handsome, the kind that all males secretly strive to be, despite whatever they may say. During his time as a nymph, Rowan had been well-aware of the proper way to behave, he just simply chose to ignore it. He likely could have learned something from Kellen, had he not been so wrapped up in his own affairs.

Rowan slunk back into the throne room and once again approached the doorway to the underworld. He stood above the rectangle, *The Book of the Dead* in hand, and closed his eyes, speaking in tongues into the vibrating hole in the ground.

Smoke began to billow out of the doorway, and the red light began to radiate with an angry glare. Suddenly, figures that resembled humans floated out of the hole, partially transparent and emanating a greenish glow. They were men—humans who tromped through the Forest long ago, wearing torn, tattered petticoats from a distant time, and pointed tricorne hats upon their heads. There were five of them, and though their upper halves were focused and easily looked upon, from the waist down their bottom halves seemed to simply fade away into nothing. They were ghosts, and enraged ghosts at that, willing to do anything necessary to uphold the negativity they enacted on the very Forest they inhabited the outskirts of so many years ago.

Rowan stood before the five ghosts. An evil smile cracked the sinking flesh of the corners of his mouth. He did not need to speak to these specters; they could feel the emotions brewing within him. He pointed towards the entrance to Nymph Palace. The ghosts nodded, and flew straight through the wall, out of the palace, and into the Forest.

Rowan watched as the ghouls rapidly floated away. Once he could no longer see their greenish auras, he rubbed his hands together and laughed, knowing that he had sent out enough opposition to buy him enough time to begin his plan for destruction of the Higher Spirits.

The multi-species army moved quickly through the Forest, trying to make the best time possible from the Elder Triage home back to Nymph Kingdom. As they walked, they discussed their different experiences in dealing with negative entities, whether it be by learning about how to destroy them during their warrior studies or actually facing up against one, as Narena and Kellen once did. Eleonora listened to Felix's parents' experiences intently, holding Felix's hand and smiling at him as she heard tales of their accomplishments during the falling.

Myso and Basil walked towards the rear with Kellen, keeping an eye out in every direction for any potential threats.

"Want a ride, Eleonora?" Basil offered. "I bet you could use a rest, after all you've been through."

"Thank you so much for the offer, Basil," Eleonora replied, "but I'm happy to walk with Felix."

"I'll take that ride," Narena chimed in. "If that's all right, of course."

"Certainly!" Basil replied. "Hop on!"

Narena climbed onto Basil's back, happy that she could now eavesdrop on her son and Eleonora as the group traveled. But Felix caught on to his mother's sneaky behavior, and tried his best to keep his voice down when talking to the faery. Upon realizing that her eavesdropping efforts were in vain, Narena decided to take matters into her own hands.

"So, Eleonora, how did you two meet?" Narena asked with an enormous goofy grin.

"Mother!" Felix cried out, embarrassed.

"I'm just asking a simple question, Felix. She doesn't need to answer if it makes her feel uncomfortable. And anyway, I wasn't talking to you." Felix harrumphed.

"Aw, you are so kind, Narena! I'm happy to tell you about how Felix and I met!" Eleonora replied, a smile upon her face.

"I would love nothing more!" Narena replied, beaming uncontrollably as she jumped off Basil's back and caught up to Felix and

Eleonora.

"Your face is going to agonize you later if you keep up that smirk," Felix muttered under his breath, and his mother turned to him and playfully smacked his arm.

"Don't talk to your mother that way, Felix," Kellen broke in.

"Sorry," Felix mumbled. Garmon snickered.

"Now, Eleonora, do continue," Narena said.

"Well," Eleonora gushed, "Felix and I met on our first day of warrior training. He was the only nymph stationed in Troll Kingdom, and I, curious as I am, had to know why. So I asked him, and lo and behold, found out he was your son. We got to talking, and found that we had quite a few things in common. It was a lifelong friendship from there!"

"How lovely! What is it you have in common?" Narena inquired, the grin still crusading across her face.

"We both enjoy animals, we are fond of other beings besides our own kind, we love adventure, and we are very serious warriors."

Garmon rolled his eyes and sighed loudly.

"Well, in that case, Eleonora, you and I have quite a bit in common as well," Narena replied happily. She walked beside Eleonora and put her arm around her.

"That's wonderful!" Eleonora exclaimed, and Felix turned to exchange a glance with his father—who was trying not to smile—though his eyes were solely focused on the direction the group was venturing.

"There's more than just that!" Felix interjected.

"What else?" Narena asked.

"Well, what I really love about Eleonora is that she really understands me. I feel like I grew up a little jaded about my peers, since I never had any brothers or sisters. Before I met Eleonora, I never had anyone who understands what I'm thinking without me saying a word. It is like we connect on a different level, spiritually or something. She is everything to me."

Felix felt his face flush red, even more as his mother, Myso, and Basil all collectively cooed in excitement over his words, then burst into laughter. Felix glanced at Eleonora, who was looking back at him dreamily, and the two exchanged a loving smile, not breaking their glance from one another until they heard Garmon's grumpy voice.

"Shh! Will you all shut it for a second? I think I hear something!"

Garmon halted in his tracks and the rest of the army followed suit. He held up his hand to silence them as he peeked around a bush. Luckily for the small beings, the bush was just thick enough to provide them a hiding spot as the branches began to emerge from the trunk of the bush just around their ankles.

The creature that Felix and the faeries had witnessed just before they dashed into the underground tunnels was pacing around through the trees, outside of the sacred clearing where Felix had taken Eleonora to view the butterflies emerge from their cocoons just days ago. It seemed as though an eternity had passed since then.

The creature heaved as it moved, clumps of matted, pungent-smelling fur dropping from its body to the Forest floor as it bumbled about.

"Oh, no. It's the creature we saw by the black oak," Eleonora whispered to Felix.

"It probably followed our scent or something," Felix replied in a hushed voice.

"Don't forget, aim for the third eye!" Myso hissed.

"Everybody ready for battle?" Kellen said quietly, and everyone fervently nodded in return.

Garmon motioned for everyone to hold their weapons at the ready. All obliged and pointed their aim at the creature, who was beginning to move in their direction.

The smell of the massive beast grew stronger, and all could hear its gasping breath and feel the heat of its presence as it drew nearer. Finally, Garmon gave a signal, and one by one they burst forth from the bush, charging madly at the creature.

Garmon emerged first, soaring his spear towards the center of the creature's eyes. He had been aiming for the third eye, but the creature moved slightly, causing the spear to graze its forehead instead.

"Gah!" Garmon shouted in dismay. He raced towards his spear, which had fallen upon the ground, and picked it up to prepare his next blow.

Myso stormed towards the creature next, brandishing his own spear and getting slightly closer to the beast than Garmon was able to. He released his spear in a perfect arc, the tip of the arrowhead landing between and slightly above the creature's eyes. The beast howled and covered its face with its hands, trying to pull out Myso's spear while still protecting its face from any further attacks. Kellen saw the opportunity and released arrow after arrow, slicing off a section of the creature's ear and landing one directly into the back of the beast's hand.

"Felix, this is your chance!" Kellen shouted at his son.

Felix quickly followed his father's lead. The split second that the beast moved his hand away from his third eye to coddle his wound, the nymph carefully landed an arrow directly next to Myso's spear, which was still protruding out of the beast's forehead.

The second hit caused the creature to fall to its knees. It wailed in agony and raised its grotesque head to the sky, howling a final time before its body shook uncontrollably and burst into a deep crimson flame. It disintegrated into ash and smoldered into the dirt, leaving behind only Myso's spear and Kellen and Felix's arrows. A blackened outline of the creature was scorched into the soil, the only remaining evidence that, just a moment ago, there had even been a negative creature standing before the army at all.

Myso thought for a quick moment, then dove to the ground next to the outline, scooping up a handful of the ash that remained on the ground. He tore off a corner of his tunic and wrapped the ash up, tying the top so as not to spill any of the creature's remains. He shoved the little bag into his pocket, muttering an incomprehensible incantation to himself.

"What are you doing?" Garmon asked him.

"I just feel like we should throw whatever remains of this creature back into the underworld with Rowan," Myso replied.

"Did Magus say to do that?"

"Not necessarily, but I'm going off my intuition."

"I am certainly not one to question such a thing," Kellen broke in. "If your intuition says to do it, then do it."

Kellen looked to his wife, but she was gazing blankly at a tree, seemingly daydreaming, despite the fact that the time and place was wholly inappropriate to do so.

"Mother? You all right?" Felix interrupted her thoughts.

Narena twitched slightly and blinked her eyes, holding them shut for a brief moment.

"Honey?" Kellen asked, placing his hand on the small of her back. "You okay?"

"Yes, yes, I'm fine," Narena said hurriedly.

"What happened?" Myso asked. "What were you looking at?"

"It's so strange," Narena said quietly. "For a moment there, I could have sworn I saw Hawthorne, plain as day, just sitting on that low branch of that tree there. He said that Myso was right to collect the ash. We need to put it back in the underworld with Rowan."

"Isn't Hawthorne dead?" Eleonora whispered to Felix, who nodded.

"We need to keep moving," Garmon interjected, "lest we victimize ourselves any further."

"Garmon's right, for once," Kellen agreed. "We must continue on. That beast was nothing compared to what I feel is in store for us."

Garmon started to stomp off, and the group followed suit. Myso walked beside Felix and discreetly handed him the little bag from his pocket.

"I don't know why, but I feel like I should give this to you," the troll whispered. "Something tells me that you're the right person to hold on to this."

"I can't argue that," Felix replied, stashing the ash in his own pocket.

"You should be in charge of collecting the ash from all the rest of the foes we face before we destroy Rowan," Myso said.

"How many more do you think there are?" Felix asked.

"Now that's something I wish I knew," Myso chuckled. "Guess we'll just have to wait and find out."

Chapter 20

owan's anger boiled as he sat upon his throne, pondering the recent events and plotting what he intended to do next. He was aware that any action taken upon the army of beings he inherently knew would return to try and stop him would subsequently shape the future of his time spent in the Forest realm. He had struggled, immensely, to reach the point of being able to sustain an existence within the realm of the Forest, and had not forgotten the trials and tribulations he withstood in order to be where he currently was—sitting upon his rightful throne, in his ignorant father's place.

Rowan thought about Caul, his now deceased head henchman, and though he was currently incapable of feeling sympathy—or really any positive thought for another being—he did feel sorry for himself. He was now at a loss for a reliable second-in-command, particularly one that harbored the same negative intentions as he did. He remembered when he had first come across Caul, shortly after emerging from the underworld. Rowan had been wandering through an unincorporated section of the Forest where no kingdom could reside, just outside of the darkest, most sinister part of the Forest when he came across the goblin.

Caul had surprised Rowan by popping out of a bramble bush and hissing at the former nymph, threatening him with his drooling fangs. Rowan had quickly knocked the goblin to his knees and loomed menacingly over his fallen body.

"What a pathetic creature you are, Goblin," Rowan had said. "You'd be a much more formidable opponent had you learned better ambush tactics."

"I only know what is inherent in my nature," the goblin had rasped. "I thirst for chaos, though I have learned much in the way of deception by way of Doppel."

"I can show you what chaos is like," Rowan had replied, "But in return you must submit to my demands. I am not of the living beings of the Forest, therefore cannot be destroyed as such. I will control you, but together, we can control all of the Forest."

"What is it you need of me, master?" the goblin had asked.

"I need you to gather all your goblin brethren. If you fully give yourself to me, I can guarantee you power over the beings of light within this Forest, the ones who for generations have persecuted you, and sent you away to live in the darkness, and shown you no love, sympathy, or even mercy. Do you wish revenge upon these beings, and the Higher Spirits who have allowed this fate to befall your kind?"

"Yes, yes, master. I shall do what you wish of me," Caul had replied, frantically nodding his head.

From that point on, Rowan had stayed with Caul, showing the goblin all that he would need to know in order to fully become a being of darkness, and went over his plans for destroying the barriers between the underworld and the Forest realm with his new main henchman.

The memories of the goblin now plagued Rowan, and the thought of Caul perishing saddened him, in a way, though it was not for the sake of the goblin whatsoever. It was the fact that now, without the aid of Caul, Rowan was essentially on his own. He would have to finalize his original evil intentions for the destruction of the Forest, and of the Higher Spirits themselves, alone.

Rowan's mind then raced back to the time of his death, as the falling was really beginning to wreak havoc upon the Forest just a generation ago.

After perishing as a nymph, Rowan had awakened to find himself floating through what seemed to be a swirling vortex of lights, pulsating between white and red. The colors would shift and fade into and out of each other in a never-ending pattern that caused Rowan's head to spin. White, red. White, red. He was being pulled, so flapping his arms to control which light he was floating towards was futile. Finally, the colors boomed at him, then sucked away to leave nothing but the pure blackness of space, and though he heard nothing but silence, he could feel a presence glaring down upon him.

Rowan, I'm afraid your time in the Forest has ended. Come with me, and I will prepare you for your next opportunity to live...

A calming, yet assertive voice resounded over the silence, loud and echoing; yet Rowan quickly realized that the voice was booming within his mind, and when he tried to hear it with his ears, found he could not.

Why are you speaking to me? Rowan thought furiously. *My father once said that Higher Spirits are forbidden to speak to living beings.*

You are no longer living, Rowan, the voice replied. *You are in another realm now, one not controlled by the laws of the Forest realm. My consciousness to the Forest is slumbering because of Gorgon, though my presence is here before you now, in this transitional realm. I am imparting* thoughts into your conscious mind, not truly speaking.

What is it you want from me? Rowan thought back.

Before the voice—presumably the Yew—could respond, another voice, this one much more sinister, interrupted the conversation between the former nymph and Highest Spirit.

He is mine! I caused Labete's fall. I sent Agrimon upon him. I caused this being to perish, so he belongs to me!

Rowan could not ascertain from where the looming negative presence was emanating, but for some strange reason found himself more drawn to the second voice than the first. He was still overcome with the emotions surrounding his death, and could not shake the feelings of anger, anguish, and the thought that he was somehow wronged as a nymph, leading to his eventual demise. He had been set for leadership, on his way to becoming king. Then fate stood in his path, ending his existence and stealing his opportunity to rule. Rowan could not fathom an afterlife of light. If he was to avenge his soul and complete the destiny he felt he deserved, he would need to do it himself.

I do not wish to enter the light. I have unfinished business in the Forest, so I choose to remain in that realm until my soul is vindicated, Rowan said. He chose his thoughts carefully, as he knew they would dictate what would become of him.

This is what you choose? Then it shall be. You will receive no help from the Higher Spirits of your Forest, and you will remain in the underworld unless you can muster enough energy to manifest yourself into your realm, the calming voice resounded in Rowan's mind once again.

Why can I not just haunt the Forest? Rowan implored.

You have a choice. To move on, into the light, and forget your time as a nymph in the Forest forever. You have chosen the darkness, and with that comes the denial of your freedom of will. If you must pick up the pieces from this life, you will never learn how to make things better in the next. You will be sent to the underworld, where you will be shown no mercy, the Yew replied.

Don't listen to the Yew, the sinister voice—who Rowan assumed to be Gorgon—said. The underworld is just the place for you. There you will ready yourself to enact retribution upon the beings who failed to save your life.

You are wrong, Yew, Rowan thought angrily. Mercy will be shown to me, as I demand it. But I cannot promise I will bestow any upon the beings who will experience the wrath of my revenge. I will not rest until I have destroyed all who failed me, and the entire Forest will beg for mercy at my feet.

As Rowan finished his last words to the voice, the blackness of the abyss began to recede into obscurity, and the red, pulsating light returned with a vengeance, blanketing the nymph. He felt the overwhelming negative presence of the second voice, speaking to him as he soared through the red-colored vortex.

You have chosen the darkness, Rowan. You will follow my demands, and I will spare you from the torture of the underworld beasts. The Higher Spirits must be destroyed, Gorgon's voice boomed from all directions.

What is it you want me to do? Rowan replied within his mind, trying to hide his thoughts of his own vindictive agenda. He had already resolved himself to the idea that he would return to the Forest realm, in spirit form, to influence his father enough to awaken the Yew and destroy Labete. Once Labete was out of the picture, then Rowan could muster up energy for his own vengeance on the Forest and the Higher Spirits.

You are the son of a king. That alone gives you power. Use the negative emotions you feel to conjure up enough energy to stop those who oppose me. Haunt them, and destroy them before they can reach me or awaken the Yew's consciousness to the Forest.

I will, Rowan lied, and was immediately thrust into what looked like a damp, dull cave, with jagged rocks stabbing out of every angle, and the pulsating crimson light that vibrated varying depths of red. He slammed into the dirt face first, slumped on the ground for a moment, and listened to the anguished screams and wails surrounding him before slowly raising his eyes to witness the sight of the hellish underworld.

Gruesome beasts and writhing creatures tromped about, encircling Rowan, and licking their lips at the sight of the fresh meat of a newly fallen soul. A few approached him, sniffing around, but something about the fallen nymph seemed to repel them.

He finally arose, and glared at each beast directly in the eye, lunging at the ones who came too close, until they all finally scattered.

When a being of the Forest is banished to the underworld, those sent with evil already boiling within their hearts are more likely to grow into monstrous beings when engulfed in the negativity of their new realm. Overwhelming emotions, such as anger, helpless despair, and hatred have the opportunity to overtake a soul, and when combined with the imminent negative influence of the location, reign supreme in one's overall consciousness.

Rowan was by no means an evil being yet, at this point in time; but he certainly was not innocent of the emotions that begin the process to create a negative entity. When Rowan realized his eventual fate, he submitted fully to the darkness. He didn't simply allow himself to be overtaken by the negativity—he vowed within his rotting mind to be the best at it.

Shortly after entering the underworld, Rowan had been visited by none other than Doppel, the Under Spirit of deceit. Doppel had shown Rowan how to go about controlling goblins, as the Under Spirit was eager to increase the numbers of his physical likeness in the Forest. Rowan had been unsure of Doppel at first, due to the Under Spirit's duplicitous nature, but found out quickly that Doppel wanted nothing more than to help the one Gorgon favored to enact the chaos the Undermost Spirit so desired in the Forest. So Rowan had learned all that he could from Doppel, and readied himself for his eventual entry back into the Forest realm.

Rowan suddenly snapped back to reality, trying to remember what had happened after he interacted with Doppel, but found that, try as he might, his mind would not recant the events following his fall into the darkness. He knew that, during the falling, he had successfully manifested himself to Kellen, and later to his father, prompting him to awaken the Yew. But he would need to really dig much deeper within his mind if he wanted to remember how it was that he eventually escaped the clutches of the underworld and into the Forest realm where he currently resided, not just as an apparition.

It had been a generation since he had fallen into the underworld, and he had been able to manifest enough energy during the time to appear as a specter more than once. But what had happened since then, and how had he been able to enter the Forest realm completely—not just as a negative entity, but as a rotting, solid existence? Perhaps it was Labete's demise that granted him additional power. Or perhaps he had taken a fated opportunity when it was presented to him. All Rowan knew now was that he was no longer in the grasp of anyone but himself, and if the Higher Spirits were to be destroyed, now was the time to begin the process.

CHAPTER 21

The multi-species army was growing closer to Nymph Kingdom, and though they were near their destination, all were aware that the possibility of facing another minion—or multiple minions—was growing more and more imminent. Garmon continued to lead the way, and had forbidden the group from speaking amongst each other as none of them had the desire to draw any additional attention to the group.

The army had been following a deer path, an easy and straightforward way to navigate the various kingdoms of the Forest. The deer were wanderers, always looking for the next best shrubbery or grassy field to munch upon, and their constant movement—plus the desire to revisit areas previously trimmed by their jaws—had created solid, thin paths throughout the Forest that inadvertently allowed the smaller beings of the Forest access to pass through areas surrounding the kingdoms with rougher terrains.

The deer path ahead of Garmon looked clear, and Felix found himself surprised at the notion that perhaps they would reach Nymph

Kingdom unscathed. But his thought was extremely short-lived, as a grayish, humanoid figure writhed straight into their path, sliding on its stomach and hissing at the small beings with an opened mouth full of jagged, rotting teeth. They screeched to an immediate halt, and withdrew their weapons once more.

"Prepare to fight again!" Garmon called out, and the group all readied their weapons.

"This one smells better, but is much uglier if you ask me," Felix joked to Eleonora, who managed to muster out a quick giggle despite her obvious nervousness.

The creature rose to its knees, lengthening its spine and coiling its lower half around, like a curled serpent ready to strike. It reared back and forcefully spat directly at the army, causing them to leap backwards in unison and gather closer together. The saliva of the creature seeped in the soil, hissing as it decompressed into the dirt. One drop of spittle landed on some moss that was lining the side of the deer path, and the area of the plant affected immediately died and withered away.

"The saliva is venomous! Do not allow it to spit on you!" Narena shouted at the army.

Kellen hurriedly ripped a thick strip of bark off the stump of dead tree nearby, and placed it as a barrier between the army and the creature. The group quickly ducked behind the bark, with a being emerging every few moments to shoot an arrow or sail a spear over in the creature's direction. Myso grabbed a satchel and pulled out a few of the extra thorns that had been saved earlier in their journey, and frantically secured them to some twigs he found along the Forest floor.

Basil slipped off to the side of the path while his comrades fought with the writhing creature, scurrying through a few bushes to get a closer glimpse of the army's foe. The creature was very distracted, as it tried to fend off the arrows and spears soaring its way, so Basil took the chance to back his rear end right up to the side of the creature without it noticing.

Just as the creature realized what was happening and turned its grotesque face to see who was sneaking up on it, the skunk released a spray of musk with a powerful force that he had not previously known in his lifetime. The creature was knocked off guard, and fell to its side, wailing and covering its seething eyes, as if Basil's musk had burned them out of their sockets.

"This is our chance!" Garmon yelled. "Go!"

Basil looked over to see his comrades simultaneously charging at the fallen creature, who was spitting blindly into the air, disoriented. Garmon tried to hover just close enough to aim his spear at the third eye, but before he could complete the shot Felix leaped out of nowhere, wielding a short blade, and landed directly on the creature's forehead, slamming the blade down precisely into the creature's third eye.

The gruesome underworld creature howled and thrashed around. Then, just like the hairy beast, it burst into flames and smoldered into ash, seeping down to the depths of the Forest floor, leaving a scorched mark on the land.

Myso, once again, scrambled to collect some ash from their fallen foe, and wrapped it up in a little tunic bag in the same manner as he had with the hairy beast. Felix rushed over to grab the bag once it was tied tightly, but as soon as he put it into his pocket, Garmon came right up behind him and gave him a good shove.

"Foolish nymph! I would have landed the shot if you hadn't gotten in the way!" Garmon shouted angrily. "You think you can just run willy-nilly through every battle and come out a hero? I'm the leader of this army, and I should get the best shots!"

"Willy-nilly? If anyone here is willy-nilly, it's you, Garmon!" Felix cried.

"You're willy-nilly! Stay out of my way," Garmon replied.

"The creature would have spat its venom right at you had I not intervened!" Felix snapped back, frustrated that Garmon could even fathom yelling at him for saving his hindquarters.

"Stop it, you two! It doesn't matter who wielded the final blow. The creature is destroyed, and we mustn't lose ourselves over something so trivial. We are an army, and Garmon, if you want to continue leading us, you would do best to hold your tongue," Kellen said.

"Your only desire is to defend the honor of your family! Felix is capable of being wrong, you know," Garmon retorted.

"I am capable of being wrong! My father is simply trying to say that I am not in the wrong now!" Felix nearly shouted back.

"Felix, desist! Garmon, that is enough!" Narena shrieked, and the two stopped, finally, their mouths agape over the frustration in the female nymph's normally soft, caring voice. "You're *both* willy-nilly! And whoever said that being willy-nilly was something to be ashamed of?"

Kellen rushed over to his wife and put his arm around her, rubbing her shoulders to calm her down. Eleonora shuffled over to Felix and stood beside him, glaring back at Garmon to prove her point.

"Mother, I have tried time and time again to make peace with Garmon. But he will not yield! I know not of what to do anymore!" Felix protested.

"Felix, the Forest is full of differing personalities. Both of you need to understand that you're not always going to get along with everyone you're forced to be around. But in this situation, you have to work together, whether you like each other or not. Sorry, son, but that's life!" Narena smiled at her son, and attempted a smile over in Garmon's direction as well, despite the fact that she, too, was irritated at the male faery.

Narena did not want Felix to see how annoyed she also was at Garmon, but instead look upon a mother who was able to put her own personal feelings aside for the betterment of the group, and act morally rather than instantly upon a fleeting emotion—even though Felix's annoyance at Garmon was anything but fleeting.

Garmon looked surprised for a brief moment, then cracked the tiniest of half-grins on the corners of his mouth back at the endearing, seasoned nymph, much like he had to the former Nymph Queen, Tiatana. Perhaps if Garmon had submitted to his affinity for females who were much older than he, as he seemed to prefer, the love triangle between the two faeries and nymph would have ceased to exist, and the current situation would have been much different. But Garmon was prone to suppress any true feelings of his that didn't span from an accepted sentiment, so whether or not Garmon did in fact enjoy the wiles of an older female was irrelevant.

"I am willing to put this behind us if Garmon agrees as well," Felix replied. Narena glanced at the faery, who was nodding with his arms folded over his chest.

"Good. We have much more important things to worry about. And, by the way, if any member of our group can be accredited with victory over that creature, I would suffice to say that it would certainly be Basil." Narena beamed at the skunk.

"I agree!" Myso declared, and patted his good friend on the back.

"Aw, shucks, fellas, it was nothing, really," Basil replied, stammering through his words and seeming slightly embarrassed.

"All right, now can we all finally agree that it's time to continue on?" Kellen said in his deep, masculine voice, to which the army collectively cheered as loudly as they were able to without being noticeable.

The army moved on, and continued to venture down the deer path in the direction of Nymph Kingdom. Garmon noticed, as he walked ahead of the group once again, that in all his excitement over his argument with Felix, he had not realized that a small droplet of the creature's saliva had landed on his left forearm. It must have happened during the time he was hovering above it, trying to land a shot.

The spittle had seeped through his flesh, leaving a deep red scorch mark in the shape of an actual teardrop cascading down his forearm. It felt hot on his skin. When he touched it gently, it shot a painful electric jolt through his entire arm and shoulder, and burned with a pulsation that the faery simply couldn't ignore.

Garmon decided not to tell his army about his wound, as they were sure to hassle him about it, and instead picked up two wide, thick, dark green leaves and wrapped them around his wrists, creating cuffs that he could explain were for better spear-throwing accuracy. He had never before experienced such an injury as a warrior, and didn't know what to expect from the wound, but decided it would be better to trudge on with his quest rather than cause any false alarm over a mere scab. Garmon just hoped the wound wouldn't persist any further—at least until they had ensured Rowan's destruction.

CHAPTER 22

s the multi-species army drew closer to Nymph Kingdom, the pain in Garmon's forearm became almost unbearable. It throbbed, in a pattern almost like the tune of a song. Its rhythm coincided with every careful, quiet step the faery took as he ventured to what he now believed was surely their certain doom. The scab was almost speaking to him, giving him a foreboding sense of the macabre destinies the army was sure to face in the near future.

The army approached the outskirts of Nymph Kingdom, and every individual within the group began to feel a sinking pit in their stomach, the kind one feels when free-falling from the branch of a tree, or off a particularly tall rock. Narena—by far the most sensitive to matters of intuition—nearly toppled over from the horrible feeling, so her husband walked alongside her, keeping his arm planted securely on her waist to prevent any further lapses in equilibrium. Felix had felt a similar but less prominent sensation than his mother, but he was adept at hiding any physical weaknesses due to his intense warrior training. He refused to visibly allow any of the army to witness the emotions he felt within his body.

Felix acted towards his intuitive feelings in a similar fashion to how Garmon hid his recent venom wound, and yet both were so irritated with one another that they certainly would not be apt to notice any type of similarity between the two.

"Are you all right, Felix?" Eleonora whispered as the two walked along together.

"I'll be fine. I just have a really bad feeling," Felix replied.

"No talking," Garmon interjected, though not bothering to turn his body around as he walked.

"Sorry," Eleonora said quietly.

The army had reached the creek that spanned along the boundaries of Nymph Kingdom—the very creek Narena frequented daily prior to the falling and the current haunting, and the same creek that Felix grew up spending time around with his mother, hearing her stories of her salamander friend, Hawthorne. All were aware that they were growing closer and closer to their destination, and that thought alone was enough to worry them.

When they reached a make-shift fox hole located near Kellen's childhood tree home, the army ducked inside so they could rest for a moment and mentally prepare themselves to enter Nymph Kingdom.

Everyone sat down except Myso, who stood above his comrades, hovering around Garmon especially. The troll opened his mouth a few times as if he were about to say something, but each time quickly shut his mouth and stroked his chin, as if delicately searching for the best possible way to share his current thoughts. Finally, he spoke.

"I'm afraid most of you may not be keen on this idea, but I feel as though it's imperative I suggest it. I think we should separate once more," the troll said, sounding slightly unsure of himself but maintaining the assertiveness in his voice that the group was now well-acquainted with.

"What? Why?" Garmon interrupted, before the troll was even fully able to finish his thought.

"Well, hear me out now. If Rowan is planning an ambush for us, it would be wise to do everything in our power to avoid it. We know that Magus is waiting for a mental stimulant from us through divination to begin his spell. I think we should split off, with some of our group focusing on clearing a safe pathway for a few others to reach the palace without any interruptions. Some of us can work on battling all of Rowan's minions, while the others can bypass all those battles and just go to Rowan himself."

"So, who did you have in mind to fight the minions, and who would face Rowan?" Kellen replied calmly.

"I feel as though it should be Felix, Garmon, and Eleonora to face Rowan. The rest of us can provide ample distraction to any adversaries we could possibly meet along the way," Myso said. "And remember, Sator directed us to kill Caul so that they could make it to Rowan unscathed. It should be them, I'm sure of it."

"Well, I can't argue with that," Garmon chimed in, puffing out his chest slightly. "I mean, if a Higher Spirit directed it, it must be entirely accurate."

Felix couldn't tell if Garmon was being sarcastic or not. He narrowed his eyes at the faery, willing him to make his statement more comprehensible, but as usual Garmon gave no indication of whether or not he was being serious. Insulting a Higher Spirit was strongly frowned upon in this Forest, and though the falling created a bit less confidence in the abilities of the Higher Spirits, the beings of the Forest were still encouraged to worship and trust in them. Felix knew that the Under Spirits would stop at nothing to influence the beings of light against the Higher Spirits, but felt at this time it wasn't entirely necessary to start up another argument with Garmon again. So he kept his mouth shut.

"Myso's right," Narena broke in. "I, too, have seen a version of the final battle within my mind. But I only see Felix and Eleonora. No one else."

Garmon harrumphed. "Of course."

"All right, then, let us rest for a short while more and we will continue on together until we meet another foe, then we will go our separate ways," Kellen said, as his wife snuggled up next to him.

Myso walked to the very back of the fox hole and sat down, cross-legged, and meditated, asking for love, guidance, protection, and direction from the Higher Spirits in the remainder of the army's quest. Swirls of colored mist danced around his body as he fell into the depths of his consciousness, and drifted off into a golden-glittered white abyss where he floated weightlessly for a moment. Then he began to see within his mind's eye a silhouette of a quadraped—a lean, hoofed outline with towering branched antlers, formed out of a thick, white mist that shimmered with golden glitter. As Myso focused his mind on the silhouette before him, he began to see more and more details of the outline's physical features. It was, in fact, a deer's presence that stood before him, and Myso needed not to venture into the depths of his mind to know who it was that approached.

Sator, I thank you for hearing my pleas. We need your direction, now, more than ever, Myso fervently thought, and was delighted to see that the Higher Spirit seemed to be listening intently.

Sator's head nodded once, and the right hoof kicked out and arched back in, as if the Spirit were doing all possible to vocalize agreement without actually exerting the necessary energy to speak. Speaking by Higher Spirits was forbidden in the Forest realm, and doing so resulted in weakness that could very possibly lead to the Spirit's demise.

Myso emitted the thought to Sator that he did not want the Higher Spirit to speak, as all the energy that would be used to do so was much better suited going towards the Spirit's main purpose: to direct.

Sator drew closer to Myso, despite the two floating in a meditative abyss, and when the Spirit was an inch from the troll's face he began to feel jolts of electricity within his body, as if the Higher Spirit was charging him up for the tribulations that were inevitably to come. Myso's mind began to fill with images of what would possibly happen, shown through Sator's projection of the images into his thoughts. As an image faded into view, the troll noticed that he could see right through it, as if it was a ghostly projection of an event already recorded into the Forest's history.

Myso saw Felix, standing triumphantly over Rowan's fallen body, his spear raised high above his head, with Eleonora happily standing beside him. Garmon was laying on the ground just off to the side of the two—slightly moving so the troll knew he was still alive, but barely so. It looked like the battle with the transformed nymph of darkness had taken a toll on Garmon's body. The troll ascertained that his intuition about separating the members of the army had been correct, confirmed by the direction of the Higher Spirit.

The image faded away, and a new one slowly began to appear in its place. Myso then saw himself, Basil close to his side, waging battle against the armies of Rowan's goblin minions, amidst piles of scattered goblin bodies. He noticed Narena and Kellen, badly beaten up but still standing, fighting with all their might against their gruesome foes. Myso found himself drowning in the image of the direction Sator was showing him, and tried to take in every minute detail so he could be sure that he would be doing exactly what the Higher Spirit was recommending he do. He knew that this vision was not entirely set in stone. Any slight changes in the events leading up to those visions could alter the eventual outcome.

Sator then shot back, as if transferring the energy had caused him pain, though Myso was informed enough about Higher Spirits to know they were incapable of such feeling in their Spirit forms. As Sator's image slowly faded away into obscurity, Myso drifted back to his consciousness, resolving to himself that he would use Sator's energy wisely, and very aware of the fact that he would surely need it.

Rowan scanned through the yellowed pages of *The Book of the Dead*, his ancient, unabridged text that delved into all matters of the Forest realm, written long before *The Forest Grimoire*. He aggressively ripped past pages of magical spells that were of no use to him now. He knew there had to be a way to weaken and destroy the Higher Spirits—or at least a way to strip them of their power and immortality, thus enabling him to destroy them as he would a living being of light. After all, isn't that what had happened to Labete? So it must be possible to do it again, without the aid of the Higher Spirits casting one of their own into mortality.

The book told of weakening a Higher Spirit by encouraging them to speak, but Rowan couldn't imagine that a Higher Spirit would ever respond to a spell he performed. He would need to ambush one somehow, perhaps by using a being of light as bait. Once the Higher Spirit appeared to save the helpless being, Rowan could somehow prompt it to speak and weaken it enough that it would fall from grace, become mortal, and subsequently be destroyed by the once-nymph's own, rotting hands.

"Yes, that should work quite nicely," Rowan spoke aloud to himself. "I shall bribe Sator using a precious, innocent, little nymph. Surely that will prompt the Higher Spirits to take notice. Obviously I was not innocent enough to be saved of my harrowing fate, so if the Spirits decide to take action over one of my adversaries, that will be just one more reason to exterminate them completely, one by one."

Rowan was very aware of the fact that a group of small beings, including a few nymphs, would be arriving at Nymph Palace very soon to attempt to destroy him. He snickered to himself as he thought of capturing a nymph who was set on ending his reign, and using that being to tempt one of the Higher Spirits to the palace to meet its own demise.

The Higher Spirits seemed to be sensitive to the nymphs. Perhaps it was because of their inherent obliviousness the Spirits found them endearing; or maybe it was that nymphs were prone to be very dedicated to their roles within the Forest; but for whatever reason, the nymphs held a special place in the eyes of the Higher Spirits, and seemingly, always had. That very well could be the reasoning that led up to Labete's own demise—that the Higher Spirits thought so highly of the nymphs that the Under Spirits felt they could use the Higher Spirit's sensitivity to the nymphs to their advantage, so had Agrimon possess Labete and have him choose the most foolish, ignorant nymph he could find to be the next Nymph King. The Higher Spirits would have much preferred a nymph king who was more sensitive to the needs of others, not just one's own species, and that alone was enough to turn their backs on one of their own.

The nymphs were important, for some reason unbeknownst to them, or any other being of the Forest for that matter. They wielded a power of will that most nymphs were completely unaware of. Essentially, the nymphs had a way of tying all the kingdoms of the Forest together. If Nymph Kingdom fell, the rest of the Forest's kingdoms would follow suit, and then eventually so would the rest of the Forest.

And if the Forest fell by way of the haunting, then the Higher Spirits could cease to exist, allowing the Under Spirits to reign supreme.

Rowan's sunken eyes caught a glimpse of some text on a page explaining the origins of the different beings of the Forest. He scanned it, quickly absorbing the descriptions of the different Higher Spirits, the negative entities that lurked within the Forest and the underworld, and the different beings, like faeries, gnomes, trolls, and nymphs. The section describing nymphs really caught his attention, and as he read, he began to learn much more than he ever had about his former kind.

"The Nymphs as the Proto-Elementals: Origins of the Forest Beings," he read aloud.

According to the book—which explained not just matters surrounding the dead, but also all ancient aspects of the Forest—nymphs came long before faeries, gnomes, or trolls. In fact, the other beings of the Forest were actually derived from nymphs, evolved long ago in ancient times by way of varying necessities of life in the different sectors of the Forest.

Faeries had originated from a kingdom of nymphs who evolved to have wings for the purpose of living up higher in the trees. It was just an added bonus that they found they were able to adequately watch over the Forest and see danger approaching for miles from so high up. Perhaps this was why they carried such an air about themselves. The faeries felt like the guardians of the Forest—and in a sense, they were—yet such an imposition created by choice was surely not something to go bragging about. But faeries were closest to the nymph's bloodline, as they had evolved from nymphs the most recently, (though still very long ago,) as more and more troubles began to plague the Forest, and the need for more specified and additional guardianship was required. According to the book, they were known as 'arboreal elementals'.

Trolls were coarser and more ornery nymphs that grew larger over time from living in expansive rock quarries, and spending extensive amounts of time in and around mountainous regions, searching for precious jewels and metals. They acted as the muscle behind the official entrance to the Forest realm, as their kingdom was located right on the outskirts. Any being or entity looking to enter into the Forest realm would surely need to bypass at least one station of guarding trolls—possibly the entire kingdom—before entering into the kingdoms of the animals or smaller beings of the Forest. The time spent in the rock quarries had made the trolls a bit grumpier than other beings, but that trait also made them extremely powerful warriors and protectors of the Forest. The book referred to them as 'mineral elementals'.

And finally, gnomes came from a very small kingdom of early nymphs who were specified to care for the earth itself, so were born wise to the matters of the Forest, but also looking as though they had already aged for decades, hence the beards. In fact, even female gnomes were graced with the wisdom of a beard, though theirs were far less prominent and were likely to be joked about by other beings rather than admired. Gnomes were the true thinkers of the bunch, and their knowledge and sapience had been passed on from not only generations upon generations of gnomes, but imparted to the earliest gnomes by the Higher Spirits themselves. There were not many gnomes still existing within this particular Forest, and the ones that still resided within the Forest boundaries tended to keep to themselves, the very last of the 'earth elementals' within this Forest.

All of these beings, whether wise, powerful, or headstrong, derived from nymphs at one point, a long time ago. In a sense, nymphs were the beginnings of the beings of the Forest, the alpha species of all the beings of light, and that is very likely why they were so favored by the Higher Spirits despite the fact that in general, nymphs didn't typically over-excel in any particular arena. But the book even stated that Higher Spirits were more likely to be summoned by the likes of a nymph, and that in all their innocence and obliviousness nymphs harbored a power unrealized by their own kind. One could even be used to weaken a Higher Spirit enough to cause it to fall from grace—that is, if paired with the correct incantation.

Rowan tried to remember if he had learned of this ancient history in his studies when he was a being of light, but found, to his dismay, that he could no longer recall any aspect of his living time that wasn't a source of his vengeance. Overall, however, it was likely that he hadn't, because faeries were surely the type to eradicate any information they felt was incriminating from all the history books, and demand the other kingdoms do it as well. And since nymphs were so eager to please, they complied with the faeries' demands in order to keep the peace.

Rowan slammed *The Book of the Dead* shut and stroked his matted hair, which was once blond but now was caked in mud, blood, and some other form of sticky filth. As he pressed into his head, the skin of his scalp slid out of place. He quickly righted the placement of his hair upon his skull. No sense of decay was going to rain on the former nymph's parade. He snickered with excitement at the thought of the vibrant beings that would storm his palace set on his destruction, only to be met with an ambush of spiritual proportions. Not only would he destroy the beings who were inevitably on their way, but he would use them as bait to perform a more sinister deed—destroy any Higher Spirit whose weakness he could exploit.

"Come to me, and destroy me, I dare you," Rowan said aloud, followed by a booming laugh that echoed through the walls of the palace. "Your good intentions will prompt your own demise, and the further destruction of your own beloved Higher Spirits!"

The former nymph sat back on his throne, cackling as he located the page in his book that would instruct him on how to summon a Higher Spirit that was not in a state of slumber. He read over the incantation repeatedly, memorizing it within his rotting mind. He still tore out the page and pocketed it, just in case he would need to reference it later. He then located the page with the complicated incantation that, along with the bait of an innocent nymph, could cause a Higher Spirit to decline. But then he spotted another incantation that interested him.

"*How to invoke the power of an Under Spirit*," he read aloud. "Hmm, this could prove to be very useful."

The former nymph continued reading, and when he had completed the section he put the book down, quickly rushed to his father's quarters, and returned with a handful of herbs and a large, putrid-smelling black ant. He crushed the insect into the herbs and set the concoction aflame, his head tilted to gaze down at his feet.

"Under Spirit Doppel!" Rowan called out, his voice echoing through the palace room. "Doppel, I invite thee to possess my being with your power of deceit! Invoke unto me a part of your energy so that I might destroy all those who oppose me!"

Rowan felt a strange entrance of energy into the room, and suddenly a jolt of electricity shot up his spine. He heard no words, neither aloud nor in his mind, and assumed it was because Doppel did not want to chance weakening himself. But Rowan inherently knew that some of the deceitful energy of the Under Spirit had been imparted into his rotting body, so took a slow, deep breath, and righted his shoulders as he did his best to absorb as much of the Under Spirit's power as he could. Then he went back to memorizing the incantations.

Once he could recite the two incantations to himself without referencing the book, he quickly ran back to his father's quarters and emerged moments later with a small sack of mixed herbs—the same mixture left over from when Alston had helped awaken the Yew. Rowan added in some additional necessities, and some other living ingredients he needed for the spell. The ingredients included a jar of strange, annelid-like creatures resembling worms with spider-like legs, which were clearly still alive, wriggling around in a never ending panic within the glass.

Rowan returned to his throne, and practiced the spell over and over in his head. Now all that was left for him to do was sit and wait for his sacrificial nymph, who was surely on its way, innocently unaware of the former nymph's plans for the destruction of an individual of his own kind; a living, breathing being of light, one of his former flesh and blood.

CHAPTER 23

"Rest time is over," Garmon demanded. "Everyone get up, it's time to go."

The group gathered themselves and followed the male faery out of the fox hole. Garmon said nothing as he led them towards Nymph Palace, and continually turned around to make sure they were staying quiet as well.

His forearm throbbed, a pain that he now found to be quite the distraction. With each pulse of the wound he noticed his thoughts began to drift in and out of negative feelings about his quest. Part of him no longer cared about saving the Forest, and instead wanted to focus on his own feelings of anger and jealousy towards Felix. It was as if he had split into two beings within his mind, with one urging him to continue his journey and save his Forest that he'd sworn to protect, while the other was prompting him to only care for himself, to abandon his army and wander off into the Forest alone. Go back to Faery Kingdom, where he would never feel that he was second fiddle to a nymph, especially one who did everything in his power to make Garmon's life as difficult as possible, including stealing the heart of the female he loved.

As his vision threaded in and out of the Forest path ahead of him, Garmon began to panic. His eyesight was failing; the venom must have spread through his veins. Garmon could still see the path in front of his body, but now there was an apparition that appeared to be attempting to manifest itself before him.

The specter was long, very skinny, and dull gray in color, surrounded by a blackened mist. It loomed across his pathway, saying nothing to the faery, but maintaining a menacing presence about itself. Garmon recognized this phantom as a goblin, but something about its appearance seemed different. This presence was so minacious and sinister in nature, Garmon could only assume that it was the Under Spirit that showed himself in the likeness of a goblin—Doppel.

Garmon tried his best to ignore the looming figure before him, but he found as he continued walking that no matter how close he got to the specter, it always stayed quite a few steps ahead of him, though imminently near and omnipresent nonetheless. Eventually Garmon grew used to seeing the phantom before him, and just decided to continue on his way to Nymph Palace, whether Doppel decided to join him or not.

Just as the group was about to cross the threshold into Nymph Kingdom, a flaming ball of scorching magma came whizzing through the air in the army's direction, driving into the dirt just inches away from Garmon's feet. He leaped in surprise, then, upon hearing Kellen shout for the army to duck behind a log nearby for safety, realized that he was still standing in broad view of whatever was firing at them, as the rest of his comrades had immediately followed the nymph's demands.

"Garmon! Get over here!" Myso screamed at the faery, as another fiery ball slammed in the dirt just in front of the log. Garmon stared at the troll, eyes glazed over for a moment, then suddenly snapped back to reality and darted behind the log to join the others.

"Where is it coming from?!" Narena shouted, as another fireball whizzed past the log and smashed into a tree behind them, setting a few of the lower branches on fire.

"It has to be in front of us!" Kellen replied. Fireballs were being sent in their direction one after another, wailing a high-pitched hiss as they soared through the air.

Myso slowly peeked up over the log and saw, to his dismay, that a horrifying creature had emerged from behind the particularly thick trunk of an oak tree that was within the confines of Nymph Kingdom. It was enormous, much larger than a human, and glowing with liquid magma that seeped out of a thick, black crust that engulfed its entire body. The troll quickly ducked behind the log again, and the words trembled out of his mouth as he described the creature who was currently attacking, amidst the wails and explosions of the fireballs that were continually being thrown in every direction surrounding them.

"It's only a matter of time before the beast's aim is true! We must defend ourselves!" Kellen screamed, and leaped up over the log to snap an arrow at the creature's face.

The arrow sliced through where the creature's nose would be, but immediately caught on fire and sank into the depths of the beast's lava face, disappearing from view without having any effect whatsoever on the adversary. Despite the first shot's failure, Kellen continued to loose arrows in the direction of the beast, but each time his arrows were simply sucked into the abyss of the creature's liquified body.

"I'm going to run out of arrows if I keep this up!" Kellen shouted. "Narena! Help me distract the beast! Everyone else, surround it from all angles and wage a full-blown attack!"

Kellen continued to leap out over the log and pretend as though he was still shooting arrows at the beast. It grinned a boiling orange-and-red smile as it swirled its fingers towards its palm, causing the flaming ammunition to appear. The beast then quickly fired the balls at the log in a quick, repeating sequence. Myso, Garmon, Felix, Eleonora, and Basil crept away from the log quietly, ducking as low to the ground as they possibly could, and fanned out around the trees and bushes that encircled the battle site. When all were in their positions, they quickly scanned each others' locations around the beast, then Garmon raised his spear high in the air to signify the start their collective attack.

"Myso, you go first!" Garmon declared, and the troll nodded in reply.

Myso charged out of his hiding spot behind a nearby tree, followed by Basil, who ran backwards at the beast, jumping up slightly to spray his pungent odor directly in its face. Myso ran through the mist of Basil's scent and leaped upwards, piercing the point of his spear directly into the creature's third eye. The magma beast screeched, as the spear was sucked into its body just as Kellen's arrows did.

Garmon quickly followed the troll's attack, flying straight at the beast and violently stabbing his spear perfectly next to the remainder of Myso's spear that was still protruding from the monster's face. Meanwhile, Felix and Eleonora were slashing their blades at the creature's ankles, slicing off the crust that kept the magma confined within the beast's body. As the crust was scraped away, the magma began to slosh from the creature's body and seep into the Forest floor, making the beast significantly shorter, and providing a better opportunity for multiple third eye shots. But as the magma began to form a puddle around the sinking underworld creature, Felix and Eleonora were forced to retreat from the ground to the top of a rock nearby, and eventually so were Myso and Basil. Garmon was now the only member of the group who was well-equipped to wage a full-blown, final attack upon the monster, and seeing the opportunity to finally be the hero of the group that the faery always knew he was, Garmon was happy to oblige.

The faery grabbed the blade secured to his ankle, and pulled back slightly before shooting his entire body directly at the wailing beast's face. He slammed his blade perfectly between the monster's eyes, right in between what was left of his and Myso's spears. The creature howled, and the ground trembled as the last of the crust slid off the magma, glowing red before sinking completely into the puddle on the ground, then finally steaming into ash which began to blow away with the first few gusts of a blustery wind.

Felix jumped down from the rock, hastily scooped up some ash from the ground before it blew away, and put it in his bag. He pocketed the bag and helped his comrades tiptoe around the magma that was spilled across the ground in order to retrieve their weapons that hadn't been melted down by the magma's heat. He then wasted no time approaching Garmon.

"I must say, Garmon," Felix said confidently. "You really showed your warrior nature just now. Allow me to be the first to congratulate you on bringing down that beast."

Garmon looked Felix dead in the eye but did not reply. Instead, he merely nodded politely to the nymph and started to walk back down the pathway to Nymph Palace. Felix exchanged some confused glances with the rest of the group, but shrugged his shoulders and started to follow the faery once again.

Garmon's arm was once again throbbing, though he noticed that the pain had seemed to cease for the duration of the battle against the magma monster. He discreetly peeked under his leaf bandage to assess the current state of his wound, and found it had grown substantially larger in the time since it had occurred. A yellowish-gray pus was beginning to seep out of the original contact site, and the wound itself was a deep crimson red that was black around the borders. It had now crept up and around his entire arm, pulsating underneath the rotting skin as it throbbed.

Garmon was horrified by the sight of his own arm, and quickly covered it up once again, nearly keeling over in pain at the moment the leaf bandage touched the wound. His eyes darted around to see if anyone had noticed his affliction, but luckily, no one had. He quickly reached under his tunic and felt around his chest area to confirm to himself that the chain around his neck was still intact. It was. Then he surveyed the path ahead of him, wondering if Doppel was still lurking ahead of him, taunting him as he had before. He wasn't.

The group crossed the threshold into Nymph Kingdom, tiptoeing quietly and running from a bush to behind a tree, then behind a bush once more. Garmon and Kellen peeked out to get a good look at the entrance to Nymph Palace, then ducked their heads back out of view to instruct the army of their next move.

"There are at least six goblins patrolling the entrance to the palace. Two are just mere steps away from our position, while the other four are pacing around the entrance to the palace and the foyer," Kellen said. "Myso, Basil, Narena, and I will charge out first and begin to fight them. When all the goblins have come to battle the four of us, then it will be time for Felix, Garmon, and Eleonora to sneak past us, into the palace. If the goblins notice you three, you might need to fight them. Is everyone ready?"

"Yes, that we are, Kellen!" Myso declared, and Basil nodded his head fervently in accord. Narena beamed at her husband and rubbed his back. Felix and Eleonora held up their blades triumphantly, but Garmon was too busy frantically tying thorns to twigs, creating two spears for Myso and himself to replace the two that were now lost to the depths of the lava monster. The faery handed a spear to the troll, and, ignoring Kellen, motioned the army to begin to storm the palace.

Myso charged first, shouting a war cry that immediately drew the group of goblins' attention to him. But Basil was not far behind his troll friend, and softened the blow upon Myso by squealing a high-pitched skunk call that caused one of the goblins to focus upon him instead.

Basil slammed his body into the goblin that had rushed him, and began spraying all forms of musk upon his foe, all the while slashing his razor-sharp teeth and claws in the goblin's general direction. He felt his claws scrape flesh, and a sticky warm liquid drifted down his forearm and seeped into his fur. Basil knew he had gotten a good swipe, and continued to squirt musk until assured he had disarmed his foe. Then in one brief snap of his jaws, the ever-so-kind and gentle skunk bit forcefully into the goblin's neck, sawing through his muscle and vertebra, spilling the darkest of red blood all through his thick, coarse, black-and-white fur, and eventually decapitating his adversary. It was only when he heard the thud of the goblin's head upon the ground at his feet did he desist his raging attack, looking around briefly then rushed over to three goblins, who had clustered together to battle Kellen and Narena.

Myso watched his friend's small victory out of the corner of his eye as he battled his own goblin foe, and though slightly disgusted by the actual scene of witnessing a decapitation, was impressed by Basil's true abilities as a warrior, which had been fairly hidden up until this point.

"Remind me to never mess with you again, my dear friend!" Myso jovially shouted out to Basil as he fought.

"And don't you ever forget it!" Basil yelled back, as he continued to fight amongst Kellen and Narena. "I know where you sleep, Myso!"

Myso only had a moment to chuckle aloud before he was completely engulfed in his own fight. His goblin was a swift one, and each time the troll attempted a vicious jab it would just narrowly miss an area that was sure to perish the foe. The goblin sneered each time Myso missed, which caused the troll's mind to spin out of control in frustration. Myso had to keep mentally assuring himself to remain patient, for if he were to upset himself over missing a possibly fatal blow, it could very well end in his own.

Then an idea came to him that, prior to this moment, he had never once pondered before—surprisingly so, since, in the troll's opinion, it was brilliant. Myso quickly enacted his plan, which consisted of him slightly pretending to be upset over missing a weakly executed stab at his adversary, then when the goblin took a brief moment to laugh at the troll's failure, Myso pulled back his spear and, using all the strength he could muster, jabbed it directly into the goblin's heart. The goblin gasped, looked Myso straight in his lavender eyes, then gulped its final breath, slumping onto the Forest floor with one final gasp. Myso wasted no time in looking down upon his fallen enemy. Instead, he rushed over to the cluster of goblins that was currently plaguing his friends, and began to fight once more.

Four remaining goblins fervently battled against Kellen, Narena, and Basil. As Myso rushed over to help his friends, he saw that Felix, Eleonora, and Garmon were delicately sneaking from their hiding spot into the palace, just out of the goblin's view. Felix and Eleonora made it inside without being seen; but just before Garmon could also drift out of view, one of the goblins—a particularly hefty one that had been fighting Narena—lost interest in the female nymph and instead, focused his attention on the faery.

The goblin shrieked and charged straight at Garmon, who looked shocked for a brief moment before clenching his spear tightly in his hand, looking the goblin straight in the eye, and charging right back at him. He delivered a powerful first blow, stabbing the goblin in the shoulder with his right arm while his left jabbed his blade into the goblin's lower back with a force previously unbeknownst to the faery. He ripped his weapons from the flesh of the goblin, who looked to be in utter shock. Before the goblin could even deliver a counterattack, Garmon stabbed with his weapons again, this time slicing the blade upwards to create a gaping gash right through the torso, causing the goblin to wail in agony.

Garmon continued his annihilation of his foe, stabbing and slicing as blood sprinkled the ground, littering the trees and bushes that surrounded their battlefield, and covering the entire ventral side of his body in the dark, sticky liquid. Garmon certainly would have continued his attack long after the goblin had already perished if it weren't for Narena, who surprised the faery by coming up behind him to gently let him know that he had already destroyed his foe. *Destroyed* was an understatement, in fact, because not only was the goblin destroyed, but currently in front of Garmon there was little evidence that there had previously been a living being battling him at all. There was only a pile of grayish, blood-stained flesh that lay pathetically in a clump, seeping into the soil.

Garmon blinked his eyes rapidly, stared down at what once was his enemy, then angrily shook Narena's hand off his back, prompting Kellen—who, of course, had taken notice—to abandon the goblin he was currently battling to rush over to defend his wife.

"Get away from me! I'm supposed to be in the palace!" Garmon snapped in a raspy voice unlike his own, his eyes unfocused, and stormed away from the battle scene towards the entrance to Nymph Palace.

Kellen grabbed his wife, pulling her further away from the already-departing faery, as Garmon had now proven himself to be too unpredictable for Kellen to risk having his kindhearted wife anywhere near. He made sure Narena was all right before he grasped her hand and led her into the battle against the goblins once more. There were currently three left, and Myso and Basil were handling them well. When Narena and Kellen re-entered the battle, the nymph couple quickly stabbed another one through the heart. Now there were two goblins left.

Myso thought the battle was nearly over. The two goblins were beginning to look terrified of their inevitable fates as they fought against the troll and skunk. But perhaps the goblins were sensing something of their own sinister nature, as a horrible thickness began to engulf the air around the scene of the battle. A mist started to form around the beings as they fought, pulsating a greenish glow that transformed into shapes of humans that once were.

The five ghost men slowly manifested into appearance, surrounding Narena, Kellen, Myso, Basil, and the two goblins. Myso continued fighting his goblin, sneaking a few quick glances at the stoic yet sneering faces of the ghost men who cackled at the sight of the battle scene without making a sound. Just as Myso slammed his spear through the heart of his goblin and watched him fall, he noticed that the ghost men had moved in closer, and as Basil finished off the last goblin with a forceful swipe of his jaws, the ghost men were even nearer.

"We're being surrounded, keep together!" Myso shouted to his comrades, trying to hide the bit of nervousness that was apparent in his voice as the ghost men closed in further on them.

Narena, Kellen, Myso, and Basil drew closer to one another, facing outwards with their backs to each other, holding their weapons at the ready but all unsure of exactly how to fight against the ghostly adversaries, who seemingly bore no weakness that the army was aware of. They could try to wield attacks upon the ghouls' third eyes, but these appeared to be intelligent manifestations of humans that formerly were, not negative entities that crawled out of the underworld, nor even a former Higher Spirit, possessed by an Under Spirit, who fell from grace to the clutches of mortality.

After Kellen released an investigatory arrow perfectly through the third eye of one of the ghost men without so much as a flinch from the specter, the group ascertained that different measures would be needed to combat their current foes. In his mind, Myso begged for the Higher Spirits to help Felix and Eleonora; and as the ghost men advanced towards the army, his last thought was for Magus to hear his plea, and begin the spell to close the doorway to the underworld.

CHAPTER 24

elix and Eleonora rushed through the foyer of the Nymph Palace, through an ornate hallway, then finally into the palace throne room. There, Rowan sat upon the throne, decrepit as ever, rotting away while still bearing a knowing, sinister look on his face, as if he had been anxiously awaiting their arrival, longing to quench his thirst for their demise.

Felix stopped, and Eleonora skidded to a halt behind him. Both stood before the gruesome former nymph who had enacted the destructive haunting upon the Forest. For a brief moment, Felix even thought to himself that actually making it to the point of facing Rowan was easier than he had anticipated. But his thoughts were short-lived, as he was now, finally, standing in front of the adversary who had uprooted his and his friends' and family's entire existences *and* caused the haunting in the Forest.

"I see you've finally made it. Took you long enough," Rowan sneered, baring his yellowed teeth and blackened, drooping gums to the pair.

Felix brushed Eleonora further behind him, puffed up his chest, righted his posture, and readied his spear.

"You've tortured this Forest long enough, Rowan. I can no longer allow you to turn the light of the Forest into your perilous darkness," Felix said forcefully.

"That, Nymph, is where you are wrong. It was I who was tortured by the Forest, forced to be a casualty of the Forest's evolution. For harmony's sake I was sacrificed, so because of that I will end harmony," Rowan replied, his eyes piercing into Felix's soul. "But first, I'm going to need that spear, if you don't mind."

Rowan raised his arm, holding his wretched, rotting hand palm up in front of him. He squinted his eyes, muttered something to himself, then curled his fingers inward. Before Felix even knew what was happening, his spear flew out of his hand of its own volition, across the room, and into Rowan's hand. Then the former nymph repeated his gesture, this time drawing Eleonora's spear to him as if magnetized. Rowan laughed, snapped the spears in half against his leg, and tossed the pieces aside.

"The Higher Spirits will help us!" Eleonora burst out from behind Felix, and faced Rowan standing proudly next to her love.

"Ah, a nymph who actually bears some intelligence. The Higher Spirits will, indeed, help you, but at their own cost. Yes, call them to your aid!"

Rowan jolted up out of the throne and shot across the room with supernatural speed. He snatched up Eleonora up by the scruff of her neck, whipping his body back towards the throne and pulling her just out of Felix's reach.

Eleonora shrieked in terror as Rowan's grip tightened and his pointed fingernails sliced into her flesh. Felix started to rush towards the throne, but Rowan quickly grabbed his jagged blade out of his pocket—the very same blade used to slay his own father—and held it against Eleonora's delicate throat. Felix gasped, stepping back cautiously.

"That's right, good. Back away, Nymph, or your girlfriend gets it," Rowan cackled.

"Leave her alone, Rowan. She's not the one you want. Take me—what would you want with a female anyway?" Felix said calmly, looking Rowan directly in the eye.

"Oh, I can think of a few things. I was a nymph once too, remember?" Rowan licked his lips as he eyeballed Eleonora up and down. "Not that I am even capable of experiencing the pleasures of the flesh in my current state," he chuckled, "but I can certainly try."

Eleonora flinched and cried out helplessly, causing panic to race through Felix's mind. This was the female he loved, and there was no way in even the rotting depths of the underworld that he was going to allow Rowan to treat her as if she was not the most precious being in all of the Forest. Because to Felix, she indeed was, and no nymph—nor any being or entity of any realm of existence—would prevent Felix from beginning the rest of his life with her.

"If you so much as even think of her inappropriately, I can guarantee that when I get my hands on you, you'll wish for me to send you back to the underworld. It would be a welcomed vacation from my clutches!" Felix shouted. Rowan ignored him, continuing to gaze at Eleonora.

Just as panic threatened to overtake Felix, Garmon appeared out of nowhere, bursting into the throne room and charging straight at Rowan. The former nymph tossed Eleonora onto the throne and stood in front of her, slashing his rusty blade at the faery. But Garmon was extremely wound-up, angered by Rowan's control over a female he once loved, and the throbbing pain in his forearm that had driven him out of his right mind.

Garmon seemed to lose all sense of reality as he assaulted Rowan, managing to get in a good jab at his decaying flesh before Rowan grabbed him by the arm, swung his body around, and cleaved his blade downward in a sharp cutting motion, shaving down the faery's back.

Rowan sliced up Garmon's wings in a few swift movements. Garmon wailed in pain as he watched his most revered aspect of his faery existence be destroyed. The remnants of his wings cascaded in shreds down to the stone floor, silently whispering a final goodbye to the source of their reverence as they fell.

Garmon's eyes unfocused, a rage brewing inside him at the loss of his faery identity, and he saw only red pulsate through his vision as he continued his attack *sans* wings, stabbing Rowan one more time just above where his heart would be—if he were ever so graced as to possess one.

Rowan was surprisingly quick to counter back, slashing through Garmon's remaining flesh in one swift, unexpected movement. Rowan drove the rusty blade through Garmon's heart, twisting it slightly as he gasped for air. The faery fell, slumping upon the ground and twitching several times before ceasing to move completely.

But before his chest exhaled his final breath of life, the chain that had been hanging from his neck—the one that Garmon had always made a point to ensure was still there—tumbled out of his tunic, snapping away from his throat with the force of his fall.

Rowan stared at the amulet upon the floor for a moment, grinning in the most uneasy of manners. Then he lifted his foot and stomped his boot down upon it, smashing a mixture of powdered herbs and ground-up flower petals. It blew across the faery's body in a pungent puff of dust.

Felix and Eleonora watched in horror, frozen in their places, unable or possibly even unwilling to fully comprehend the magnitude of the current situation. They could only look at one another, across the throne room, helplessly separated but still never lacking the love that had grown for each another, prior to and during the haunting. Garmon, too, in all his arrogance, insolence, and pride, had held a special place in their hearts. A tiny piece of them had drifted away with Garmon's fighting spirit.

Rowan stood upright, and turned to wave his bloodied blade at Eleonora, who was curled in a ball upon the throne. She whimpered at the sight of her former friend's blood upon the blade, while Felix looked on. He still carried a blade secured to his ankle, covered by his boot and out of Rowan's view, but it was much smaller than Rowan's. It would have to do, though. He just needed to be patient for the perfect opportunity to strike.

"Now you must fully comprehend what I am capable of," Rowan sneered. "No being, be it nymph, faery, or troll, will stop me from achieving my rightful status as king of Nymph Kingdom. And if you try anything else, I can guarantee you will suffer the same fate as your friend."

"You will pay for what you've done to my friend," was all Felix could reply.

Rowan slowly walked over to Garmon's body, which was slumped in an awkward, contorted position upon the stone floor, and studied it for a moment. His attention was drawn to Garmon's leaf bandage, which he delicately lifted away from the faery's flesh. He peeked at the decomposing wound upon his arm, chuckling to himself before turning his attention back to Felix.

"It looks like your friend was not who you thought he was. He, too, was influenced by the darkness. It's apparent by the venom wound upon his arm," Rowan cackled.

"Whether or not he was influenced by the venom does not change the fact that he charged in here out of the goodness of his soul," Felix replied.

Felix was quick to defend Garmon, and though he was shocked by the fact that Garmon had been wounded by the venom of the creature they had fought some time ago, he would not accept the idea that Garmon's force of will to battle Rowan stemmed from anything other than his need to uphold his warrior status, for the overall good of the Forest.

Felix desperately wanted to believe that Garmon, a being he had spent an extensive amount of time with, though difficult and combative at times, was inherently good.

But now is not the time to mourn a fallen comrade, Felix thought to himself, and vowed to pay his respects after he had finished off Rowan and officially ended the haunting. And if he wanted to accomplish just that, he would need to focus his mind on how to handle Rowan, who was now rapidly approaching him.

"Sit yourself down, Nymph," Rowan ordered, motioning to the very rear corner of the throne room.

Felix reluctantly obliged, but managed to look all around him as he did. He noticed that he had a decent view of the glowing doorway to the underworld, though not a good enough angle should he need to dive in at a moment's notice, for whatever reason.

Rowan bound Felix's hands behind his back, then did so to Eleonora on the throne before retrieving from his pocket the page of his book which held the incantation and process of spell necessary to summon a Higher Spirit to the aid of a dying nymph. He cast a circle of the herbs and wriggling, spidery worm-creatures beside the doorway to the underworld. Rowan quickly snatched up the faery and threw her within the circle before stepping in himself. He clutched onto Eleonora's tunic and spoke the incantation aloud, his voice booming upwards as he stomped his feet over the writhing worm-creatures. Their insides exploded all around the circle as Garmon's amulet had, though far more messy and grotesque. The palace walls began to vibrate, then shook rigorously. A swirling, glittering white gold vortex opened up through the high, vaulted ceiling above the circle that Rowan had just cast.

Flashes of white light filled the room, blinding Rowan, Eleonora, and Felix for a quick moment before the light coiled to the floor, revealing a glowing white outline of a buck deer, glimmering in golden sparkles. Felix found it difficult to look away from the Higher Spirit, but saw the opportunity to sit upon his bound hands, sliding the binding into his boot and rubbing it against the blade secured to his ankle. Felix was finally able to avert his eyes away from Sator, and glued them instead to Rowan just as the binding started to loosen. Luckily for Felix, the former nymph kept his eyes locked upon the new arrival—the Higher Spirit, Sator.

Finally, Felix felt the binding give, and tore his hands out of his boot and behind his back once more, providing the illusion that he was still restrained should Rowan glance over in his direction. Now he just needed to wait for another chance to rescue Eleonora from Rowan's grasp. He hoped that his luck would stay with him long enough to save his love.

Chapter 25

Narena, Kellen, Myso, and Basil were surrounded by the five ghost men, who were slowly but surely closing in on them. Narena had been shoved by her husband into the very center of their cluster, but still held her blade at the ready just in case. Basil bared his sharp teeth and angrily hissed at the specters before them. Myso and Kellen stood, silently, weapons pointed at the third eyes of the ghosts who floated before them, until Myso finally spoke.

"What is it you want from us, ghost men? If you were once humans, you should have no issue with our Forest. Please, move on to your next life, leave us to fight the battles of this realm!"

The ghost men did not reply audibly, and instead imparted a faint, echoing message into the troll's mind, and subsequently into the minds of Narena, Kellen, and Basil as well.

We are trapped in this Forest realm, troll. Many years ago, in our human lives, we committed crimes of mortality in the Forest, so the Forest trapped our souls in its underworld. We are witch hunters, bound by our religion, and enacted punishment upon those who in life went against the word of our God. We are enablers of the truth, able to execute those allied with the darkness.

The ghost men then imparted the image into the beings' minds of one of their many crimes in life, the apparition Felix had witnessed many days earlier. The men, solid in body, chased the frightened young witch to the oak tree, where they mercilessly hung her and left her dead body to limply swing back and forth with the melody of the wind, a gruesome message to all other witches of the Forest.

"But ghost men," Myso replied aloud, "the witches do not cohort with the darkness. In this Forest, the witches are only partisans of light."

We know that now, but we are bound by our sins in life.

"Why are you doing this?" Narena squeaked out, though was quickly hushed by Kellen.

We were summoned out of the underworld by Rowan, he who controls the doorway to the underworld. He sent us back out into the Forest to wreak havoc upon the beings who dwell within, and to enact his plan to destroy the Higher Spirits and all those who share in their positive light. There was once a time when we may have been able to save our souls by learning the lessons in death that we failed to recognize in life. But that time has lapsed, and we are now fully controlled by Rowan. He has used our anger, despair, and discrimination to entrap us further in his clutches. We submitted to our own entrapment by failing to realize our mistakes and see our own faults. We are forever stuck here now, and eternally controlled by Rowan, unless we are destroyed completely.

"So, basically what they're saying is that they have nothing more to lose," Kellen mumbled to the group. "They will not show us mercy, so we cannot be swayed by their sob story." He looked specifically to Narena, who glanced away from him quickly, tears swelling in her orange eyes.

"I beg of thee, ghost men," Myso pleaded, "just move on. There's a light somewhere in your vision. Though it may be only as small as the iris of your eye, I promise you, it is there! Go to that light. Forget about Rowan. The Higher Spirits will forgive you for the crimes you committed in life."

I'm afraid we can't do that, troll. It's too late. We are too consumed by hatred.

"Life," Narena chimed in, "is truly fueled by love. Any existence that is lacking in love is surely not an existence worth having."

Myso watched, his lavender eyes wide, as the ghosts silently guffawed at Narena's words, but their ignorance only further strengthened a feeling of power that was beginning to boil within the troll's body. He felt himself growing more energized, electrified with the fortitude of vigor that was so recently bestowed upon him by Sator.

Myso's body involuntarily puffed up, something common for the body of a troll, but this time he felt like the energy that prompted his growth was coming from a power beyond his own. Sator had indeed infused him with the strength of a Higher Spirit, Myso ascertained as he felt a tingling within his bloodstream.

"I warn you," the troll said, now forcefully, "to desist your impending attack, or prepare to be blinked out of existence entirely!"

Again, the mouths of the ghouls cackled without a sound. Myso held his palms out and pointed them at the most menacing ghost who was floating just in front of him.

Myso felt a jolt of energy shoot up his arms, and a bright white light began to emanate from his palms. The light trembled and shook his body, and Myso found that he could rotate his hands to form a ball of light energy that he could manipulate enough to throw using both arms. He released one that slammed into the ghost man's face, creating a bolt of lightning that shot out of the ghost's third eye before splitting the ghoul straight down the middle and gulping away its existence completely. The other four ghosts looked on in horror before emitting a high-pitched, very audible noise as they all flew towards Myso.

Myso quickly destroyed another ghost in the same manner as the first before another came up behind him and knocked him off his feet. Myso slammed into the ground face first, nearly imbibing a clump of dirt, but he shook himself off and jumped back up to shoot another light ball at a ghost man who was slamming itself into Basil repeatedly. Myso's aim, true as it was, did not fail him. Now only three ghost men remained.

Narena and Kellen were huddled together, crouched low to the ground as another ghost man continually dove at them. Each blow knocked the wind out of the little beings. Kellen had tried shooting arrows at the third eye of the ghost, but found his attempts were futile so did his best to shield their bodies from the never ceasing blows.

Narena tried with all her might to enact a protective barrier around herself and Kellen, using as much of her strength and ability as she possibly could. But each time she would create a barrier, it was far too thin to fully protect the two, and the ghost man would burst through it— cackling silently along the way—while tearing it to shreds and dissolving it into thin air.

"I can't take it anymore!" Narena shrieked finally, as the blows were making her feel ever weaker with each attack.

"You miserable soul! Fight me instead, like a man!" Kellen shouted at the ghost, prompting the ghoul to turn in his direction, slamming through his body and knocking him away from Narena.

Narena shut her eyes for a brief moment, called out to the Higher Spirits to give her strength, and grounded herself for the purpose of energizing her spiritual aura enough to at least give her enough power to match that of the remaining ghost men. Then she remembered something—despite her inability to create a protective barrier when she needed it most, she was still a sage, thanks to Hawthorne.

Narena dug deep into her heart, and felt a sense of warmth surround her. In the strangest sense, she felt as though her long deceased parents were with her at this very moment, standing by her side and protecting her. She knew she was going to be okay, so long as she stuck it out. And she needed to trust in herself and her abilities, now more than ever. Maybe then she could succeed in using her gifts to the fullest.

Narena invoked the energy of protection that she had experienced from Hawthorne during the falling. She felt herself growing more energized at her thoughts of her parents and her salamander friend—more so, in fact, than from even her pleas to the Higher Spirits. Out of the corner of her eye, she began to see the outline of an upright standing caudatan, though it was a misty white color and glittered in silver specks.

"Hawthorne," she whispered to herself. "Please, help me."

Narena focused her thoughts solely on her elemental friend, and as she did so, she felt her body begin to tingle. She burst up, and heard a chanting resounding within her mind that spoke an incantation repeating over and over. She stared at her husband, who lay upon the ground as the ghost knocked into him repeatedly. Without thinking, Narena screamed the incantation at the ghoul as she threw her arms forward, sending a wave of heat energy in the form of whirling fire that shot out from her palms and surged into the ghost that was attacking Kellen.

"Get away from my husband!" Narena shouted as her attack

impacted the ghoul. "And if you are ever so blessed as to experience life again, next time treat females with the respect they deserve!"

The ghost was blown away, as if her energy prompted a wind that was able to whisk away specters. The ghost man looked at Narena's tiny little nymph body in shock, and then simply blinked out of existence with a thundering crack in a flash of green light.

Narena rushed to her husband, clutching him as tightly as she could, while Myso quickly shot two more balls of light at the ghouls, hitting both of them and destroying them in the blink of the energy illumination. But just as the flash of the last ghost man was fading into obscurity, the little beings saw a strange, transparent, floating image hovering above them.

The apparition was of a woman, fairly young in appearance with dark hair and sparkling violet eyes. Her face was kind, and hinted at gratitude towards the group as she smiled down upon them before bursting upwards toward the sky, her long white dress trailing behind her in a wisp of trickling mist.

The four beings exchanged knowing glances of what they had just witnessed, though nobody spoke a word of it aloud.

"Come on," Kellen said after the moment had passed. "We need to help Felix."

He grabbed Narena's hand and took off running toward the palace as fast as his legs would carry him, with Myso and Basil trailing very close behind.

CHAPTER 26

In the throne room, Rowan stood, clutching Eleonora in his gruesome grasp, before Sator, the Higher Spirit he had summoned to his presence. Felix still sat against the wall just a short distance away, free of his bindings but continuing to pretend that he wasn't. Felix tried to meditate and reach out to Magus in the hopes that the wizard would receive his message through the use of divination and enact the spell necessary to close to the doorway to the underworld.

Felix could only hope and trust that Magus would be savvy to his pleas. His faith was all that he could rely on now, and though he had recently lacked faith in the beings of the Forest, believing that the only way things could be done was by doing them oneself—a feeling fueled by the seemingly endless opposition of Garmon—at present he didn't have much of a choice but to believe.

Beings are inherently good, he kept telling himself, and thought of Garmon once again as an example. Despite losing the love of Eleonora to a nymph, Garmon had still stood by his oath as a warrior to protect the

Forest, and Felix certainly could not hold that against him. *He gave his life so that I could have mine,* Felix thought, *and I cannot allow him to perish in vain!*

As Felix snapped back to the situation at hand, Rowan was still dangling Eleonora before Sator.

"Come on, you lazy old buck, you," Rowan mocked the Higher Spirit. "Do something! Save your precious nymph!"

Sator said nothing. His deer face bore no expression, which seemed to only further anger Rowan.

"You call yourself a Higher Spirit! All I see is but a mere deer, able to be destroyed by a human hunter! If you have such love for the nymphs, then surely you will save this one!" Rowan spoke angrily, his own death apparent in his voice.

Sator, Arepo, and the Yew were all to blame for his demise, because had they not cast Labete from his Higher Spirit status in the first place, the falling itself might never have happened, and Rowan certainly would not have been destroyed by Labete's minions. Rowan refused to acknowledge, of course, the fact that Labete had been possessed by Agrimon.

Sator continued to give no discernible response to Rowan's taunting, except for cocking the deer head slightly to look upon the former nymph. Rowan held Eleonora directly in front of Sator, and used one of his long, sharp fingernails to scrape across her cheek, causing small bubbles of blood to surface from the gash. Eleonora whimpered and shook in terror, as Rowan then lifted up his blade and held it to her throat.

"Come on, Sator, don't you want to rescue her? She's one of your nymphs, the innocent little beings that have helped you bless this Forest since the beginning! Surely you must do something..." Rowan trailed off as he shook Eleonora around, waiting for a response from Sator.

When the Higher Spirit simply just stared back at him, he growled under his breath and began to evoke the incantation that could, with the proper bait, mortalize a Higher Spirit. Rowan boomed the words, exaggerating their sounds, speaking as forcefully as he ever had, as a nymph or as a creature from the underworld. But still, even as he jolted his nymph bait around, Sator did not appear to be weakened in any way by Rowan's words. This infuriated him, and he threw Eleonora violently down onto the ground, cracking her temple loudly and causing the faery to slide across the polished stone floor.

Eleonora wailed, and it took all of Felix's energy not to leap up and try to intervene. But he knew that this was not the right time, and every bit of his intuition was telling him to wait.

Trust in yourself that you will know when the time is right, a voice resounded within his mind. Stay put for now!

As Felix received these thoughts, he noticed Sator looking at him out of the corner of his eye. It must be Sator, then, who was directing him on what to do to save Eleonora and the Forest. The Higher Spirit did not speak aloud—he could not, without weakening himself.

Rowan screamed the incantation again, picked up Eleonora off the ground, and threw her down again to his feet. Sator remained the same. Rowan yelled the incantation again, and again, each time kicking Eleonora or otherwise harming her in some manner. Felix could almost not bear the agony of witnessing this any longer, and started to move.

Not yet, the voice ordered, and though it pained him to do so, Felix obliged his thoughts once more.

Eleonora reached into her boot and pulled out her small blade, swiping it around in the air at Rowan as he tried to pick her up again. She managed to get a good slice across his cheek, but not enough to stop his advance. The former nymph looked momentarily surprised at the attack, but quickly summoned her weapon into his decrepit hands before tossing it away.

Rowan snatched Eleonora up from the ground, and, trying to goad a response out of the Higher Spirit, grabbed her face and thrust it into his, licking his tongue out of his rotting mouth as he kissed Eleonora on the lips, smacking his drooping flesh against her vibrant skin. She gagged audibly and wailed as loudly as she could. But Rowan ignored her cries and continued kissing her for the purpose of upsetting Sator enough for the Spirit to act. But again, Sator just stared at Rowan, this time looking slightly confused.

Felix sat, his mouth agape in shock and horror, watching Rowan's disgusting attempt at hurting Eleonora, and vowed to himself that when finally provided the opportunity, he would make Rowan sorry he had ever even fathomed using Eleonora as any pawn in his sick game.

Rowan pulled away from Eleonora, tears streaming down her face as she glanced at Felix, who mouthed to her that he loved her. Eleonora's eyes seemed to convey that she felt the same way, but lacked the glisten that Felix was so accustomed to. That alone enraged Felix even more, and he knew that Eleonora had, in a manner, been stripped of her innocence.

"Why isn't this working?" Rowan complained, looking to Felix as if he could answer.

Felix just shrugged and looked away. Rowan glared at Sator, who was beginning to drift back upwards towards the ceiling, and noticed that the swirling vortex was slowly sucking the Higher Spirit away.

Then, in a flash of booming white light glittered in gold, Sator disappeared completely. Rowan fell to his knees, still clutching Eleonora, and screamed in frustration.

"Doppel!" Rowan howled. "Doppel, I need thee!"

Felix looked around the room but nothing appeared to be happening. This frustrated Rowan even more, and he dragged Eleonora over to the underworld doorway.

"Doppel!" he cried down into the endless abyss.

"Doppel has imparted some of his energy into you," a voice hissed loudly from below. "That is your gift from the underworld. You are on your own."

"It's not enough!" Rowan shouted, stomping his foot on the ground like a spoiled brat. "I need more of his power!"

"Even the Under Spirits cannot quench your thirst for greed," a different, raspier voice replied. "You could try another spell, but we have helped you all that we can."

"To be a great villain," another, booming deep voice added, "you must create your own wretchedness. You must trust in your own abilities. The Under Spirits can't do everything for you. They've taken you as far as you need."

"The Under Spirits have failed me!" Rowan gasped, practically heaving. "I've been deceived! They can only give so little, yet expect so much in return! They're impossible to please!"

"I guess if you can't trust an Under Spirit," Felix said loudly from his corner, "who can you trust, right?"

Rowan whipped around from the doorway and faced Felix from across the room. "Curses from Gorgon!" he shouted, scraping his nails down his wretched face with his left hand as he still grasped onto Eleonora with his right. "Gorgon on Sator, Gorgon on the Higher Spirits, and Gorgon on these two cursed nymphs! Clearly this disgusting strumpet of a nymph dirt-walker was not innocent enough to provide me the necessary bait for Sator's demise!"

This statement angered Felix so much that he couldn't hold his tongue any longer.

"What would you know of her innocence?" Felix snapped from his seat against the wall, prompting Rowan to throw Eleonora down and charge straight over to the nymph.

"What did you say to me?" Rowan challenged, assuming that Felix was still bound and had no means of defending himself.

"Who are you to determine if she is an innocent being or not?" Felix retorted.

"I care not if she is an innocent *being!* I care if she is an innocent *NYMPH!*" Rowan shouted, spitting in Felix's face.

"Well, I'd say that you're out of luck then. I assure you that Eleonora is not a nymph."

Rowan looked Felix dead in the eye, piercing anger giving way to complete horror at the realization of his mistake as Felix continued to speak.

"Unfortunately for you, Rowan, Eleonora was born a faery."

Chapter 27

agus was just finishing up the preparations for his spell when Rhoslina and Lorella arrived home to the Elder Triage tree. They walked in with an air about themselves, one that showed the wizard that they were well aware of the goings-on of the haunting of the Forest, and their look of concern conveyed to the wizard that they had returned quickly in the hopes of providing help.

Lorella had long dark hair with equally dark eyes—though her left eye was droopy—and her spine curled in such a position that her body was in a permanently hunched posture. Rhoslina also had dark hair, though she was blessed with sparkling, periwinkle eyes, a bump on the bridge of her nose, and a fairly large mouth for a human being. Both witches sighed as they ascertained the magnitude of the Forest's situation, despite being aware of it from the far distance to which they had traveled. They'd known it was bad, but they couldn't until this very moment wrap their minds around just *how* bad.

Magus scooted them over to the sitting room where he had already cast a circle of salt, with the herbs and crystals necessary for the spell placed delicately within it. The divination crystal sat upon its copper post next to the circle, and Lorella rushed over to it just in time to receive the repeat message from Felix, pleading for the wizard to begin the spell.

Rhoslina watched as she went over Magus's preparations for the spell, luckily noticing that he had missed a very valuable ingredient—blessed saltwater from the ocean just off the coast of the furthest outskirts of the Forest. Rhoslina rushed upstairs to her quarters to grab her personal bottle of the seawater, grateful for the little beings' sake that she and Lorella had arrived in time to help Magus perform the spell.

"If we succeed, my dear Magus, in exorcising this negativity out of the Forest, I can guarantee that you will find yourself as the newest member of our Elder Triage," Lorella beamed at the wizard as they prepared themselves for their act of magic.

"And if I am correct in my divination, my dear, I will be joining you soon enough!" Magus chuckled in reply.

"All right, are we all ready, then?"

Rhoslina briskly entered the room, appearing as though she were floating over to the witch and wizard who awaited her return. Now was the time to begin the spell.

One witch, wizard, elemental, or little being performing a spell wielded some element of magical power. But when multiple beings performed a spell—especially if the beings were particularly magically endowed—the spell was made to be even more powerful. This was something discovered during the falling when both King Alston and Nessaba the witch successfully performed spells to awaken the Yew, who subsequently went on to destroy the Agrimon-possessed Labete. Magus was aware of this recent Forest history, and thus was grateful that Lorella and Rhoslina had returned to help, as three witches were surely to be more effective than just one.

Now that the final ingredient was ready for the spell, Rhoslina instructed Magus to sit within the salt circle he had cast and begin burning the herbs, which were crushed down to a fine, pungent powder and mixed with Eleonora's faery wings. The smoke of the burning herbs wafting upwards from the open window would prompt the Higher Spirits to take notice of their spell—granted they were not already aware of the situation at hand and just waiting to be prompted through magic to take action. It was imperative that the Higher Spirits noticed, as they would essentially be providing the spiritual energy needed to close the doorway. Meanwhile, Rhoslina would chant the incantation necessary for the spell along with Magus, and Lorella would keep watch over the little beings who were currently up against Rowan in the divination crystal.

Magus set the herbs aflame, and the smoke drifted upwards to the ceiling and out the window. The wizard watched as the fog created by the burning herbs traveled out into the open air, dispersing all over the Forest. Lorella rushed into the kitchen and returned quickly with a large broom, which she fanned furiously at the window to force the smoke to travel out as quickly as possible as she continued her gaze upon the divination crystal for any changes in the situation that the witch and wizard would need to know.

Magus then began the incantation, joined shortly thereafter by Rhoslina. The wizard began to flick droplets of the blessed seawater around himself within the circle, imagining the doorway within his mind and mentally closing the door with each flick of his wrist.

"Doorway of darkness, fill with light. Trap all those who mean us fright. Stay with those who lead with love. Help us, Spirits, from up above," the witches and wizard chanted melodically together.

The wizard and witches knew that as mortal humans, their spell would only succeed in the event of the utmost and complete concentration. The lives of the little beings, as well as the overall fate of the Forest, resided in their hands. They would need perfect timing if they wanted their spell to work properly.

Lorella watched in the crystal as Rowan, still clutching Eleonora, charged straight at Felix. Felix was clearly screaming something at him, and Rowan was yelling back. Although Lorella could not fully discern what they were saying to one another, she still intuitively knew that it was not yet the right time to completely close the doorway by finishing the spell entirely. Rowan would need to be thrown into the underworld first, dead or alive, before the doorway could be closed in such a manner that Rowan would not be able to simply open it up again. They would have to wait until Felix was able to weaken Rowan enough to get him into the doorway to the underworld, and until that happened, all they could do was continue to chant the incantation to gain the spell more power, and be patient.

As the witches and wizard continued chanting, a strange, faint and far-away-sounding knocking began upon their front door. While the witches maintained their chant, Magus quickly darted to the front door to see who it was. He looked through the peek hole, but found nobody was there. So he opened the door.

"Hello, Magus."

A hunched-over woman with long, auburn hair stood proudly in the door frame, her orange eyes practically glowing on their own with every glimmer of light that shone across them. Her demeanor was similar to that of a bat, and her nose was flat and square to one's likeness. She was partially see-through, and a delicate white mist trickled around the sides of her form.

"Why, Nessaba," Magus cried in surprise. "I didn't expect to see you until the afterlife!"

"That's the funny thing about this haunting," Nessaba replied. "We're all in the afterlife now."

"Come in, come in," Magus said, stepping aside to allow the witch to enter the home.

"Nessaba!" Lorella and Rhoslina cried out in unison. "What are you doing here?"

"Don't stop chanting, whatever you do, please," Nessaba said hurriedly. "I'm here because I think you're going to need my help."

The witches and wizard began chanting once again, and Nessaba calmly walked over to their burning herbs and faery wings. She sniffed the air, waved her hand around to keep the smoke billowing, then turned to her witch and wizard friends and winked. Nessaba then inhaled deeply, pursed her lips in a perfect circle, and blew as forcefully as she could onto the flaming ingredients.

The fire erupted all around Nessaba's ghost form, blanketing her entirely with roaring flames. Then, as quickly as the fire flared up, it reared back down, allowing the smoke to rise up and billow stronger than it ever had before.

As the cloud of smoke drifting out the window grew more and more powerful, Nessaba joined the group, adding a fourth voice to the loud, chanted recitations of the incantation. After she had completed the third run, she simply turned to her friends, nodded her head, and walked out the door.

Still chanting, Magus rushed behind her, but Nessaba moved quickly enough that he couldn't quite catch up. The wizard stood in the door frame and watched helplessly as Nessaba continued drifting away, venturing further into the Forest's thick trees, until finally her image slowly dissipated into the scenery, and the witch had faded away to nothing.

CHAPTER 28

"She's a faery?!" Rowan cried, spitting saliva through the air in Felix's direction. "You insufferable nymph! I could have used you as bait instead and succeeded in destroying Sator?! You will pay for what you've done!"

"What I've done? You're the one who thought she was a nymph!" Felix retorted.

Rowan moaned in frustration and slapped Felix right across his face. Then he stormed over to Eleonora, picked her up as she wailed for Felix's help, and carried her little, wriggling body over to the pulsating red light of the doorway to the underworld and held her above it.

"If she's not a nymph, then surely the Higher Spirits won't care if she becomes a creature of the underworld," Rowan declared, dangling Eleonora above the pulsing abyss.

He laughed maniacally and looked at Felix, who was staring back in complete horror. Rowan then winked at Felix, and, with one swift motion of his rotting hand, dropped Eleonora into the pulsating red hole.

Eleonora's tiny body landed with a thud against the underworld floor, causing Rowan to cackle uncontrollably. Felix could no longer contain himself. He was as livid as he had ever been in his entire existence.

Felix leaped up, much to Rowan's surprise, and tackled the former nymph to the ground, stabbing him in the chest but narrowly missing his heart with one arm as he fended off Rowan's waving blade with the other. Felix wondered, surprised that his mind was even able to form a comprehensive thought, if stabbing the heart of an already dead being would even do anything. But now was not the time for such thoughts—or any thought, for that matter, beyond overpowering Rowan—so Felix instead tried to focus on discovering any weakness he could on his adversary by the only way he could: fighting him just as he currently was.

Rowan swung his blade forcefully at Felix, swiping across his neck and grazing his right ear. A drop of blood streamed down the side of Felix's head and cascaded down his neck, drawing the nymph's attention to the wound. Felix felt his heart race as he ascertained the closeness the former nymph had been to cutting his throat, but tried not to let his fears distract him from his battle.

Rowan angrily swung his blade again, aiming for Felix's throat, but luckily this time Felix was ready for the blow. Just before the blade swiped close to his flesh, he quickly ducked and leaped upwards, slashing his own blade across Rowan's midsection. Though he had made contact with the former nymph's rotting skin, no blood exited the wound, and Rowan barely flinched. Felix looked in horror as several maggots writhed out of Rowan's belly gash, dropping to the floor and frantically trying to scurry away.

The two continued to struggle for awhile, equally matched in strength, until Felix was finally able to stab Rowan's left arm with his blade while simultaneously punching the former nymph in the face with his other hand. But Rowan was quick to counter the punch, and grasped tightly onto Felix's arm as he fell to the ground.

The two slid across the stone floor of the throne room, growing closer and closer to the doorway to the underworld. Felix used every ounce of his strength, and prayed for any spiritual help he could get—whether it be from the Higher Spirits, his mother, his father, Magus, the Elder Triage, or his mother's salamander friend. All of his mental efforts were certainly not in vain, as in one swift and overpowering movement, Felix shoved Rowan into the doorway of the underworld.

"The Higher Spirits may not care if she becomes a creature of the underworld," Felix shouted as he jumped in after him, the two of them falling into the underworld right next to where Eleonora had landed, "but I certainly do!"

"Then perhaps you shouldn't have followed me in here. This is my domain," Rowan replied, sneering at the nymph with his rotting, yellowed grin.

The two began to encircle each other, each holding their blade within their hands. Rowan waved his around menacingly, while Felix simply held his sturdy, ready for an attack.

Rowan lunged at Felix, his blade tearing through the fabric of his pants, cutting into a small piece of flesh in the nymph's leg but not causing any crippling injury. Felix swiped back, slicing into Rowan's right arm—the arm that wielded his blade. Rowan pulled back, looked angrily at Felix, then tossed his blade calmly over to his left hand and lunged again, this time stabbing into Felix's torso. Felix howled in pain, but still managed to slash his blade across Rowan's chest, creating a shallow cut that spanned from shoulder to shoulder. Like the others, this cut also did not bleed, but it was enough to stop the former nymph in his tracks for another brief moment, allowing Felix to gather his composure.

Felix charged at Rowan, swinging his blade with all the strength he had, slicing across Rowan's neck and partially detaching his head from his shoulders. The head teetered backwards, but the rotting nymph simply laughed before pushing his head back up to its rightful position and sneering at the nymph.

Felix countered again, this time slamming his blade directly into Rowan's third eye. Rowan glared into his orange eyes, anger piercing through to his soul. Felix gazed back at his father's once-friend, and in a brief, fleeting moment, he felt sorry for him. But the moment passed, and, in one swift movement, he pulled his blade from Rowan's forehead then forcefully swung his arm around to slice through the remaining muscly flesh and vertebrae that still clung to Rowan's decrepit shoulders. Felix decapitated the former nymph completely, sharply cutting off Rowan's wail as, in quick instant, all forms of his body ceased to communicate with his mind.

Rowan's head fell upon the underworld floor with a loud thud, bouncing twice and rolling a few feet before finally resting in place, eyes pointed upright. Felix barely had time to catch his breath before something in his mind told him to look upwards, and he noticed that the rectangular doorway back to his Forest realm was slowly but surely beginning to close.

Felix glanced at Eleonora, who was lying upon the ground but still visibly breathing.

"Eleonora?" he cried with all his might. "Eleonora, you have to get up! Now!"

She stirred, raised her head, and upon seeing the pure terror in Felix's eyes, pulled herself up and made her way over to the nymph, her sweet, lovely eyes darting about the underworld in all directions. Felix quickly cut her hands loose from their binds, and the two stared hopelessly at each other.

"How are we to get out?" Eleonora said softly.

"I don't know yet," Felix replied. "I... I have to think for a moment."

"I don't think we have much time!" Eleonora squealed.

"What if you got on my shoulders, and I tried to throw you out?"

"It's too high! And then how would you get out?"

"I don't know..."

Felix panicked at the thought of remaining in the underworld forever—it was sure to ruin all of the plans he had daydreamed for himself time and time again after meeting and unexpectedly falling in love with a female faery. He thought of his future with Eleonora, the little ones he had wanted to have with her, and the life he often fantasized about that involved them growing old together. He thought of his parents: how his mother would sob uncontrollably and mourn for who-knew-how-long at the loss of her son and only child. His father would stay strong for the sake of Narena, but he would cry alone, when he knew no one would hear.

Felix reminded himself of the strange power he had felt when he had thought of his loved ones earlier whilst battling Rowan, and how it had given him the strength to persevere through the ordeal. Rowan had been defeated using simply the power of love. His thoughts of his family and Eleonora empowered him once more, and then he thought of his friends, Myso and Basil, and all the fun times they had laughed together.

Finally, Felix thought of his mother's salamander friend, and all the love and wisdom that had been imparted to him by his family and friends for the whole duration of his existence. Surely it was to be a shame that all the love and wisdom would go to waste! But just as Felix was beginning to lose hope completely—as he accepted his fate, that there wasn't going to be any way of exiting through the doorway above—he heard the sound of a familiar voice echoing down to him from the entrance far atop from where they were.

"Felix! Eleonora!"

The two looked up to see that Myso, accompanied by Narena, Kellen, and Basil, was peering down through the doorway at them. But the doorway was waning, and growing smaller by the second, so Felix's excitement at the sight of his family and friends was short-lived.

"How can we get out of here?" Felix shouted upwards. Myso gave him a helpless look that the nymph had never previously seen upon the troll's face.

If there were ever a time to lose hope, Felix thought to himself, please don't let it be now!

Up above, Narena was frantically trying to think of a way to save her son and Eleonora. She looked around the room, but to her dismay, saw nothing that could be of any use to her. There were no curtains on the windows to be used for the two to grab onto, and the throne itself would be too heavy to dangle down for the two to be pulled out upon. But then, in all her frenzy, her mother's intuition took over, and into her head popped an idea. It perhaps wasn't the wisest, best, or most practical idea, but in this very moment, it would have to do.

"Everyone," she shouted, "I have a plan!"

"What is it?" Kellen replied. "We need to act fast!"

"Let's make a being-ladder! Basil can hold ground up top and hold onto Myso's legs. Then Myso will hold onto your legs, Kellen. Then you will hold onto mine."

The group collectively looked at her in disbelief for a moment before Myso spoke up.

"Well, it's a good idea as any right now! Let's try it!"

Narena laid on her stomach next to the disappearing doorway to the underworld, leaning her body slightly downward so Kellen could securely grasp onto her ankles. Myso then grabbed onto Kellen's, and the little being-ladder was slowly led down into the underworld. Basil grasped onto the seat of Myso's pants with his teeth, and held tightly as Narena reached out her hands to grasp Felix's hands, while Eleonora held on tightly to Felix's waist. Narena shouted for Basil and Myso to pull as hard as they could, and gradually they were lifted back toward the doorway to their realm.

There was but the smallest of opening left, just barely enough for Felix and Eleonora to squeeze through at the very last moment. But just before they were pulled out of the underworld entirely, Felix remembered the bags of ash that were once the creatures of the underworld.

"The ashes!" Felix cried aloud, quickly reaching into his pocket and grabbing the bags.

His body began to drag across the stone floor of the Nymph Palace's throne room as he was pulled out of the doorway entirely. Never before had Felix been so grateful to feel the stiff coldness of the palace ground—but before he could fully enjoy the feeling of returning to his realm, he threw the bags of ashes as hard as his little nymph arms would allow, back down into the depths of the underworld.

Then the doorway closed off completely.

CHAPTER 29

owan lay upon the ground of the underworld, his head detached but still emitting thoughts in some form of unnatural consciousness. He knew he was finally dead this time, and was back in the underworld where the whole haunting had started; but having one's head detached from one's body provides a form of strange comprehension of matters not previously understood.

Rowan could still think and see flashes of the underworld around him, but lacked control over his body, making it impossible for him to get up from where his body lay. It was at this moment, just as he watched the last bit of the doorway shut away all light and hope for his return to the Forest realm, locking the former nymph into the underworld for all of eternity once more, that Rowan finally remembered how exactly it was that he'd been able to escape from the underworld in the first place.

After he had visited his father and helped prompt him to perform the spell to awaken the Yew, Rowan had been forced to return to the underworld, as his residual energy was not enough to sustain him in the

Forest realm. Rowan had wanted, more than anything, to be provided an opportunity to return to the Forest for the purpose of beginning his haunting, yet spiritual rules dictated that unless he was summoned by a living being to return to the Forest in a solidified form, he would continue to fester in the underworld. He had managed to absorb some of Kellen's energy when he had manifested to him, and he had stored that energy within himself, waiting for the exact, opportune moment to use it.

Many years later—though a length of time unrealized by the underworld inhabitants—a sudden chaos had occurred, and Gorgon himself had appeared. The Undermost Spirit conveyed the message to the creatures of the underworld that someone in the Forest was in the process of performing a very ancient spell, one that would enable a single underworld inhabitant to be released into the Forest realm. The spell was backed by dishonest intentions, and seemed to be directed more at the Under Spirits than the Higher Spirits.

This drew the attention of every monstrous creature that dwelt below the earth, and Rowan found himself intrigued by the possibility that some entity could possibly be provided a chance to escape the torturous prison. He made his way over and saw, through a vortex that projected an image onto the cave-like walls of the underworld, that a faery warrior who was stationed in Troll Kingdom had performed a very poorly-enacted spell for the purpose of drawing the love and affections of a lovely young faery warrior to his accord.

Love spells were powerful, and when not performed correctly, had the potential for extremely disastrous outcomes—not to mention the fact that any love spell performed provided the possibility for a retribution to the performer in threefold. And the fact that this spell was called out in such a general fashion to any Spirit willing to comply... well, that was just a catastrophe waiting to happen.

Because the spell had not been performed with the most genuine of intentions, a tiny crack of a doorway had been opened—enough for one negative entity to be released upon the Forest as a repercussion for the faery's ignorant spell.

Rowan had seen his only chance, so shoved a stinking, hairy beast out of his way as he crusaded to the front of the entity line, pushing gruesome monsters off to the side and lunging at any who dared challenge him, even those who appeared much larger and powerful than the once former nymph. But perhaps fate was in Rowan's favor, as he persevered all the way to the crack of the doorway and, laughing at his unexpected victory, slid himself through the opening of the underworld before it faded away. He passed briskly into the Forest realm, giggling to himself at the thought of all the horrible, vindictive things he wanted to do to the Forest and its inhabitants.

He had appeared first, in the Forest realm, in front of the faery who had inadvertently summoned him, but upon looking at the faery's shocked expression, knew that calling upon an underworld entity was not the outcome the faery had expected. Nevertheless, Rowan was extricated—by the very same faery who had perished in his attempt to destroy him, something that was important for the love spell to come full circle and negate any residual energy that would possibly be left by the enactment of the spell and the negativity it unleashed upon its failure. And that faery, who ultimately had caused the haunting of the Forest and destroyed so many lives as a result because of the lack of faith in his own, was none other than the leader of the multi-species army stationed in Troll Kingdom—Garmon.

"I didn't summon thee!" Garmon had cried angrily upon seeing

Rowan approach him. "I was trying to perform a love spell for Eleonora! Look, I have the ingredients in a necklace and everything!" The faery lifted the amulet attached the the chain that hung around his neck.

"Well, luckily for me," Rowan had sneered, "you performed it incorrectly. Your intentions were untrue, and you failed to acknowledge which Spirit you wished to help you. And since your selfishness and foolishness fueled your spell, you grabbed the attention of none other than Gorgon."

"No, it can't be," Garmon had replied. "I take it back! I take the spell back!"

"It's too late," Rowan had laughed. "The female you desire will merely take pity on your existence, and she will never love you the way you do her. For true love is stronger than any spell, even one performed properly. You are doomed to watch her fall for her true love, her soul-mate, as you desperately pine for her attention."

"How can I stop this?" Garmon had pleaded. "Please!"

"There's only one way to end this," Rowan had replied with a smug grin. "You can sacrifice your worth, or you can perish in Gorgon's name."

"That's ludicrous!" Garmon had cried. "But what do you mean by my worth?"

"Something that makes you who you are," Rowan had snapped. "Like your wings, for example."

"You're wrong!" Garmon had yelped. "My spell worked, and I'll prove it! Wearing this amulet will bring her love to me!"

"You are but a fool," Rowan had sneered. "If that vial is destroyed, not only will the love you yearn for never love you in return, nor will anyone else. Ever. Now, stay still so I can pluck your precious little wings off."

"Never!" Garmon had shrieked, and took off running, away from Rowan, until the faery was no longer visible.

Rowan's now-detached mind shot back to the present. He no longer had the luxury of time in which to ponder the beginnings of his haunting that had ended in failure. The creatures of the underworld had now taken notice of the fallen evildoer, whose head was lying pathetically away from his body, wholly unable to defend himself.

As his vision grew blurry and then finally ceased completely, all Rowan was left with was the knowledge that the gruesome beasts of the underworld—the ones he had previously controlled—were now devouring his already decomposing flesh and imbibing what was left of his soul, eradicating his consciousness, then his entire existence completely, leaving his soul to rot, like his body, in only pure blackness and nothingness forever.

CHAPTER 30

elix, Eleonora, Narena, Kellen, Myso, and Basil lay slumped on the throne room floor for a few moments, catching their breaths and finally able to rest after their harrowing ordeal. Oddly enough, it was Felix, though having been through the most recently, who was the one to rise up first, pulling his beloved Eleonora up to her feet. He turned to his parents to help them next, but found that Kellen was already up, and helping his wife do the same.

Myso and Basil followed, and the six stood before one another, no one quite knowing what to say just yet. They all stared at each other with twinkles in their eyes before gathering together in a big group hug. But upon discovering just how much blood Felix had lost in his battle with Rowan, Kellen wasted no time holding his hands over his son's body and healing his wounds. After Kellen had finished healing Felix, he turned to Eleonora and again performed his healing ritual on her injuries.

"Thank you, Father," Felix said, still a bit out of breath.

"Yes, thank you so much, Kellen," Eleonora added. "But what about Garmon? Can you heal him?"

Kellen crept over to where Garmon lay slumped upon the floor in a bloody heap. He took the faery's pulse, leaned closely over him to listen for breathing or a heartbeat, then shook his head and sadly sauntered back over to the group.

"It's too late for Garmon to be healed," Kellen declared. "He's gone."

"Oh, no!" Eleonora cried, and buried her head in Felix's chest. Felix wrapped his arms around his love and bowed his head.

"At least he died a true warrior," Myso piped up. None of them knew about Garmon's love spell attempt, or the fact that the sole cause of the haunting had been Garmon himself.

"He was a good being," Narena said quietly, "Even if he was a curmudgeon."

Kellen nodded in agreement. Then every being of the multi-species army took turns paying their respects privately to Garmon's fallen body.

"He made the ultimate warrior sacrifice," Felix added. "And for that, I am forever indebted to him. I feel terrible that we weren't really able to smooth over our relationship before he perished. I hope that his soul forgives me for the times I was wrong."

"I'm sure Garmon forgives you," Eleonora replied softly. "Strangely enough, there was a time—back when Garmon and I first met—when I thought that someday I could love him. In a weird way, almost as if not by my own will, if that makes sense. But I felt like we would be married someday, or something." She exchanged glances with Felix. "But then you came into Troll Kingdom," the faery beamed at him. "And all of that changed. Then I couldn't imagine myself with anyone else. Ever."

"I can't imagine myself with anyone else, either," Felix cooed.

Felix looked at the area where the doorway to the underworld had been. There was no longer any evidence of there having been a doorway at all; just the same polished stone ground that Felix had always been accustomed to.

What a lovely room, Felix thought to himself as he gazed around. But nothing so lovely as the beauty of Eleonora. No ornateness of a palace nor grace of nature compares to her.

Felix desired to propose to Eleonora right then and there, but decided that it probably wasn't the best time. Garmon had perished, and everyone was exhausted from the recent ordeal. The only thing the group could even fathom doing right now was having a long, tranquil, much-deserved rest.

"Well, I suppose we should all head home, yes?" Kellen spoke up through the silence.

"What about the warriors?" Narena asked. "It's a bit late for them to start traveling back to Troll Kingdom. Why don't you all stay with us for awhile, until you're rested up?"

Felix looked to his comrades and all eyes conveyed the same agreement.

"Thank you, Mother," he replied. "That sounds heavenly."

A few days after the haunting had ended in the Forest, and the beings of the kingdoms had sufficiently calmed down enough to resume their normal routines, the surviving nymphs gathered together in front of

Nymph Palace to officially decide who would become the new rulers of Nymph Kingdom. The crowd muttered with excitement as the heroes of the haunting emerged from the palace where they had met after regrouping in Narena and Kellen's home for a few days, cleaning themselves up, resting, and feasting upon meals of human-sized proportions.

Felix was dressed nicely, in chestnut brown slacks and an orange-dyed, soft tunic that illuminated his like-colored eyes, accentuating the handsomeness that was—and always had been, very apparent—but was now very endearing along with his sharp mind. Eleonora stood by his side, wearing a lovely, flowing light blue dress that had once belonged to Narena, her hair styled in a messy bob to the likes of her future mother-in-law. On her dainty little finger, she wore a stunningly elegant engagement ring, given to her a few days after her and Felix's harrowing underworld ordeal. The ring was made of copper, delicately woven around a central moonstone that was mined, forged, and designed exclusively by some of Myso's family in Troll Kingdom. In the gleaming sunlight, the ring sparkled, and all who passed by Eleonora couldn't help but notice its exquisiteness.

Standing aside from Felix and Eleonora was Narena, dressed modestly in a long, reddish-brown dress and clutching her strikingly handsome warrior husband Kellen. Felix's parents beamed with pride for their son as they stood in front of the beings of Nymph Kingdom, ready to begin the vote on who would be the new leaders of their kingdom from that moment on. Behind them, stood lifelong friends Myso and Basil, chuckling amongst themselves.

"He better get elected," Myso teased loud enough for Felix to hear. "Or I'm writing off Nymph Kingdom completely!"

"Yeah, who needs those nymphs anyway," Basil chimed in with a giggle. "They are, after all, too oblivious to accomplish anything, let alone be true warriors."

"And they don't even have wings!" Myso added. "How can they do anything without wings?"

"Hey!" Eleonora broke in. "Wings are definitely not a necessity for a fulfilling life!"

"That they are not," Felix added, placing his hand softly upon Eleonora's waist before turning to the troll and skunk. "My dear friends, I cannot thank you enough for everything you've done during our time of peril. If I had ever felt alone growing up, it was certainly made up for during my time spent with you."

"Whatever the outcome of this vote, my dear Felix," Myso replied, "I will always consider you a great leader and true warrior."

"Yes, you were born for this, my son," Narena whispered in Felix's ear.

"I have indeed been blessed, Mother. I have you and Father to thank for that," Felix replied and turned to his mother, who in turn, shifted to face him.

"I love you, Felix," Narena said, her eyes swollen with tears of joy.

"I love you too, Mother," Felix beamed.

"And it is we, my son, who have been blessed," Kellen added, patting his son on the back. "Because we had you. You have made us so proud, and you will be a great king, one that legends will be told of."

"Thank you, Father. And if I am half the nymph you are, I shall consider myself the most accomplished in all the Forest."

"You are, my dear son. More, even, I'd say! Now, it's time for you to accept your fate."

Kellen turned away from his son, and motioned to his wife, who began to address the gathering in front of them. But before the vote could begin, a tanned, handsomely fit older man ran up to the group, out of breath.

"Did I miss anything?" he asked, placing his hand upon Felix's shoulder.

"Not yet, Grandfather," Felix said, leaning back to give the man a hug. "Where have you been?"

"Oh, nothing of the utmost importance at this moment," Felide replied. "Just some unruly reebobs encroaching on the outskirts of the Forest."

Reebobs were ancient guardians of spiritual vortices found in and around enchanted Forests. They were fairly small, about the size of a troll, and resembled an evolved primate, though they bore a set of large, full-feathered wings upon their backs. They were generally known to be quite docile in nature as they peacefully guarded their vortices, and rarely came into contact with the other beings or animals of the Forest. Unless, of course, someone was trying to tamper with or erroneously enter a vortex they guarded, in which case they would respond with a full-fledged attack. When provoked, reebobs were known to react quite aggressively and, at times, in a violent manner. Ancient Forest knowledge stated that was why the Under Spirit, Valerian, chose them as his being-likeness, as reebobs were not beings to be crossed.

For many generations, reebobs had not so much as made a peep within the Forest, so Felix was inclined to assume that any indiscretion his grandfather was speaking of would be easily dealt with. He brushed off Felide's comment, and stepped forward to receive his votes from the kingdom.

"All those in favor of Felix as our next Nymph King, say 'aye'!"

Kellen called out to the crowd. But before he could even finish his sentence, an overwhelming wave of sound reverberated through the Forest's trees.

"AYE! AYE! AYE!"

"Then so shall it be! Here he is, your new Nymph King!"

Felix took another step forward as the crowd roared, and the nymph crown was placed down firmly upon his head by his father. He turned, held out his hand to Eleonora, and gently pulled her to his side.

"All in favor of Eleonora as the new Nymph Queen?" Felix cried out.

"AYE!"

"But I am not a nymph," Eleonora protested.

"You do not have wings," a male nymph called out from the crowd. "So you are a nymph!"

"I was born a faery!"

"Well, you're a nymph now," a female faery yelled. "All hail the new Nymph Queen!"

"Hurrah! The Nymph King and Queen!" the crowd shouted. "Long live the Nymph King and Queen!"

"Look," Narena called out to Felix, grabbing his arm and pointing to the canopy of trees. "A Higher Spirit is coming!"

Felix turned to look. Indeed, a white mist had begun to form among the leaves and branches of the trees just to the right of Nymph Palace. The mist thickened, and swirls of gold trickled into the silhouette, before the image exploded into a full manifestation of a white deer, glimmering in golden sparkles.

"It's Sator," Myso declared. "He must be here to accept the new king and queen!"

Sator drifted down to where the crowd had gathered, and stopped directly in front of Felix and Eleonora, gazing deeply into their eyes and kicking his hoof. He almost seemed to be smiling. Then the Higher Spirit burst into mist once again, swirling around the nymph and former faery, blanketing them in pure white and glittering gold. When Sator pulled back, releasing Eleonora from his grasp, she was left blinking as if she had just awakened from a deep slumber, and bit more glowing and sparkly than before. The Higher Spirit then focused solely around Felix for a few more fleeting moments before shooting himself up and away towards the sky, leaving only a trickling rain of golden specks to cascade gently down onto Felix's newly crowned head.

"It's done," Felide whispered to Kellen. "He's chosen your son."

"And *your* grandson," Kellen replied with a grin, putting his arm around his father's shoulders. Felide looked to his own son and beamed.

"And *my* baby!" Narena cried with glee, clutching tightly to her husband's waist. "Look at him, Kellen! He's gleaming, so vibrant and luminous!"

"He's all grown up now," Felide commented, grinning.

"And now the apprenticeship begins," Kellen said softly under his breath. "Then Felix shall rule."

And so it was that Felix and Eleonora became the rulers of Nymph Kingdom. Harmony was able to thereupon reign supreme in the Forest and all its kingdoms, blessed and enchanted by the Higher Spirits. Now all who existed within the Forest's trees, whether being or animal, could finally, once again, live in peace.

EPILOGUE

ay beyond the outskirts of the Forest, a rumbling began that shook the foundation of the soil to the Earth's very core. The atmosphere thickened, and one small area of trees tightened so much that the air simply sucked out of existence. The area slurped, pulled deeply from within, and an enormous, swirling black hole emerged out of thin air.

A reebob, high up in the trees, started to screech a warning call to all his brethren in the area. His reverberating wails echoed through the Forest, prompting all reebobs within the immediate area to his location. But upon arriving, a strange look entered the reebobs' usually bright, shining yellow eyes. Their vision became slightly glazed over, and their bodies uncontrollably pulled towards the black hole that had just opened up, as if they were being summoned to do so by some powerful yet invisible force.

The reebobs' wings flapped, and through no will of their own flew aimlessly into the black hole, seemingly lost for all of eternity. But alas, several moments later they re-emerged, the irises of their eyes now black as their pupils, their shoulders slightly more hunched than before, and their brows permanently furrowed in a maddened stare. Whatever had happened to them within the black hole had changed them, and though they were apt to defend their vortices with violence if completely necessary, something about their new appearance conveyed the message of endless terror.

The darkened reebobs took off, flying in all directions, calling out through the Forest's canopy in their normal voices to lure all their remaining kind to the mysteriously threatening black hole. Several moments later they reconvened, observing the rest of their species enter and exit the hole, changing just as their brothers and sisters had before them. When all had transformed, they gathered around the hole, chattering amongst themselves, until finally two stayed at the hole while the others returned to their respected vortices throughout the Forest realm.

The black hole vibrated slightly, drawing the two reebobs' attentions to it, yet no one nor anything emerged from its darkness. Instead, a deep, booming voice rang out from within, reverberating through the Forest's trees and prompting the reebobs to bow their heads in reverence at its sound.

"The Controllers are on their way. Prepare yourselves for their existences!"

The reebobs screeched through the Forest, hollering to their brethren who replied in kind.

Magus happened to be walking through the Forest at this very moment, and stopped dead in his tracks upon hearing the cacophony.

"Oh, dear Yew," he whispered softly to himself. His body shuddered uncontrollably, and he felt goosebumps stand upright and riddle across his skin. "They are coming."

About the Author

T. Damon has always harbored an immense passion for not only writing, but animals and nature. Her added interest in all things magical and mythical inspired the creation of The Forest Spirit series, which embodies a little bit of everything she loves. When she's not writing, she enjoys spending time with her husband, daughter, and pets at her home in the enchanted forests of Northern California.

Other Works by the Author

Writing *As* T. Damon

The Falling: Book 1 of The Forest Spirit series

The Reckoning: Book 3 of The Forest Spirit series

The Awakening: Book 4 of The Forest Spirit series
(Coming soon!)

Perchance to Dream:
"The Desperate Warrior and the Beast Who Walks Without Sound"
(Also available as a stand-alone paperback)

Writing *As* K.L. Teal

A Girl Named Dracula

Anthropoidea